BAD LIKE US

**Books by Gabriella Lepore
available from Inkyard Press**

Bad Like Us
The Last One to Fall
This Is Why We Lie

BAD LIKE US

GABRIELLA LEPORE

For Sophia and Hayden, with all my love.

EVA

The flash of the camera stuns me for a second. Yellow spots dance in my vision, and I blink them away.

"I like this one," Karly says. The glow from her phone illuminates her face as she inspects the photo. It's pitch-dark out, apart from the amber blush of the fire. "I'll send it to you, Eva," she says, tapping at the screen. "Your hair looks good."

I comb my fingers through the ends of my windswept and salt-air-frizzed hair, untangling the light brown strands. "Really?" I reach over and angle her phone so that I can see the image on her screen. I looked dazed, too bright against a black background.

Darkness crept up on us quickly. We've spent the evening around the firepit, in a cage of tall firs—all nine of us, together. The fire paints our faces with long shadows, warping expressions. Beer bottles clink, and voices are getting bigger.

"Okay, me next." Piper leans over Karly's shoulder, all

glossy black bangs and scarlet lips. "When you take my picture, have the fire just at the edge of the frame," she instructs, extending her fingers wide. "I want it to look arty."

As Karly hops to her feet and starts lining up the shot, I stand, too. I brush the sand off my jeans and step away before anyone notices. As much as I'm enjoying this newfound comradery with Karly and Piper, I think I've reached my limit. Besides, I've got somewhere I need to be. Plans that I intend to keep.

Across the crackling fire, my gaze lands on Colton—his dark hair is curling onto his brow and his broad frame is half lost in shadows. He's sitting next to Javier on salt-bleached driftwood. Their words are drowned out by the louder voices and laughter coming from the others, but the conversation looks heavy. Javier is bowing a twig, curving it into a crescent, then letting it pop back. His hood shades his face, but I can see his downturned mouth.

My friend Miles is next to them. He isn't paying any attention to them, though; he's far too engrossed in animated conversation with Colton's twin brother, Danny.

"...have you even seen the original movie?" Miles is saying. He presses his palms together and shakes his slim hands skyward. "How can a film be marketed as a reboot when it's so shamelessly inaccurate?"

Danny pushes back some of his unruly brown hair. "Miles, come on," he says. "The original sucked, and you know it."

Miles scoffs at that.

On the other side of the fire, Piper and Karly have begun the photo shoot. Karly is holding her phone high and Piper's full lips are drawn into a pout. She's tilting her head to different angles and playing with the end of her ponytail.

Only Alice catches my gaze as I slip away. She's huddled close to Noah, watching something on his phone. It must be funny because Noah booms with laughter every couple of seconds. "You're going?" Alice mouths, her eyebrows pulling together.

I nod, and she waves.

No one else seems to notice me leave; everyone's too caught up in conversations. I tap my phone's flashlight and start making my way across the beach, aiming for the tiny flickering porch light marking the log-walled lodge—our home for one more night, and the sole property standing on this little stretch of rugged Oregon coastline. Piper and Karly's shrieks of laughter drift after me as I head toward the blinking light.

Alone and away from the fire, the darkness is a little more disorienting, but I keep going. Soon, the voices fall away, and the surge and crash of waves becomes louder. My shoes sink into the soft sand as I bypass the lodge and continue along the moonlit bay, heading for the shoreline with its sea caves and rocky projection hanging over the ocean. At the water's edge, I come to a stop, and I wait in the darkness.

For him.

But the minutes keep ticking by, and the battery on my phone is already down to one red bar.

I glance over my shoulder toward the flickering orb of light emitted by the lodge. The tide is starting to come in, bringing in knots of seaweed and pebbles.

I check the time again. It's nearly midnight.

My stomach tightens. This was a bad idea. Bad, bad, bad. I shouldn't be here.

But just as I turn to leave, a bloodcurdling sound steals the air from my lungs—a strangled scream ripples over the bay.

My heart slams in my chest. I spin around, stumbling into the darkness. My eyes dart toward the glow of the lodge, but the scream came from the opposite direction, where a hollow sea cave is lost in shadows.

Somewhere in the darkness, stones click against each other and the waves *shh* in response.

I press my hand to my racing heart. "Colton?" I call.

But no one responds.

"Hey!" I try again, gripping my phone a little tighter. "Is someone there?" I sweep my flashlight across the bay.

This is a private cove, way off the beaten track, and there's no one here but us. They shouldn't be fooling around out here. Especially with the rising tide.

Gingerly, I begin heading toward the cave, moving my light over the sand and boulders that fringe the thick black ocean.

"Hello? Is everyone okay?"

Treading carefully over the slippery stones, I forge a path to the mouth of a cave. The ground is puddled with seawater, and tide pools have formed in the depressions between the rocks. I cling to my phone as I navigate a path into the hollow.

A shiver crawls down my spine. I don't feel safe exploring caves in broad daylight, let alone in the middle of the night.

"Is someone here?"

My voice bounces around the hollow, a phantom in the darkness. I move the light over the damp walls as I edge forward, my shoes slapping through saltwater pools.

And then I notice it—a phone on the ground.

"Is anyone here?" I call.

When only the echo of my own voice returns to me, I rescue the cell and wipe the damp case on my sleeve as I back out of the cave. The case is familiar, and a chilling thought nudges at the very back of my brain.

The phone's dead, but it's still warm, as though it was just in use. Whoever was in here must have dropped it without realizing. They must have left pretty fast, too.

It's not until I run my flashlight over the abandoned cell that I notice the screen is shattered.

Article by Louis Matthias

The body of a teenager was discovered at a beach in Tillamook County. Police were called to the privately owned land in the early hours of Saturday morning, April 16th, and the victim was pronounced dead at the scene.

Eight Seattle high school students are being questioned in connection with the incident. Local police have declined to comment at this time, but it's reported that a seventeen-year-old has been arrested in connection with the death.

TWO DAYS EARLIER
EVA

Karly Davis drums her pastel-polished nails on the steering wheel as she sings along to the song on the radio, her ruby-red hair fluttering in the breeze from the open window.

This is the first time I've been in Karly's car—a mint green Prius with a Starbucks air freshener hanging from the mirror and a couple of empty soda bottles rolling around the footwell in the front passenger seat.

A rogue bottle bumps against my shoe. I nudge it aside.

"So, we've been on the road for nearly four hours, you guys…"

I can hear Piper's voice above the radio as she films an Instagram Live in the back seat. I steal a glance at her in the vanity mirror. Her sleek black hair is pulled into a topknot and her silver hoops are jiggling in the breeze.

"Four hours," she says to her phone, extending her fingers wide. A myriad of silver rings glint in the sunlight. "That is no joke, you guys. But we're high energy, loving life, and down for some fun…"

Beside her, my best friend, Alice Moloi, gazes out the side window, sunlight flickering over her deep brown skin. She's fiddling restlessly with the end of her braid, probably trying to avoid the path of Piper's video. I've noticed how Alice cringes and smiles awkwardly whenever Piper points the camera her way. She keeps her long legs crossed and her arms folded around herself like a shield.

I catch Alice's gaze in the mirror and smile. When she smiles back, I cross my first two fingers. Our secret sign that we agreed on before we left Seattle. Our code for *I've got you.*

She copies the gesture, then mouths, "Danny owes us."

I stifle a laugh. Honestly, I don't think I could have faced this trip without Alice. I wouldn't have wanted to.

This isn't exactly how either of us had imagined spending our senior year spring break, heading for some remote beach lodge with this group of people—half of whom we haven't hung out with since middle school.

Along with Alice, Miles Brynne and Danny Demarco have been my ride or dies since elementary school. We spent a little crossover time with Piper and Karly when Danny was dating Piper, and I know Danny's twin brother, Colton, and his friends Javier Ramos and Noah Lauder enough to say *hi* when we pass in the hallways, but none of that warrants a group trip. And yet, here we are. Danny, Miles, Colton, Javier, and Noah in the Demarcos' Ford truck, and Alice, Karly, Piper, and I in the Prius.

"We're just a couple of hours from our exclusive resort," Piper's voice floats through the car, and I catch Alice's gaze in the mirror again. She quirks an eyebrow at Piper's choice of wording.

"*Exclusive*?" she mouths.

Alice and I don't entirely fit in with the popular cliques that Piper and Karly flit between; we prefer to coast under the radar. But when Danny and Piper unexpectedly hooked up over the summer break after junior year, Alice, Miles, and I were befriended by association. I think our entire grade was surprised by the random pairing of Danny Demarco and Piper Meyers. Even now, I still can't wrap my head around how they managed to stay together for so many months. I can't think of a single thing they have in common. But for a while, it worked. Kind of.

They officially called it quits over winter break and appeared to be sworn enemies for a little while with Piper posting slanderous videos on her socials, calling out Danny for being *selfish* and *emotionally unintelligent*. Flash forward a few months, Piper has moved on with Javier, and now that she and Danny are friends again, we all got pulled into spending spring break at Noah's uncle's beach house in Tillamook County.

"It's a completely private retreat right on the waterfront," Piper gushes into her phone, "not even open to the public yet. So keep checking my page because I'll be posting sneak preview pictures of my luxury cabin over the next few days."

My brow creases. *Luxury* is not how this place was described to me.

But I'm excited. Judging by Noah's social media, the Colton-

Noah-Javier trio regularly drive out to the coast to surf and wakeboard, and it looks like they have the best time on these kind of trips. My dad taught me how to surf when I was a kid, and I get a little jealous when I see their pictures sometimes. I secretly want to be out on the water with them.

"Love this." Piper starts miming the words to the song playing on the radio, moving one hand in time to the beat whilst holding her phone in the other. She flips the camera toward Alice for a second, and, right on cue, Alice cringes. When the camera is back on Piper, Alice finds my gaze in the mirror and widens her warm brown eyes. "Send help," she mouths slowly.

I grin in response.

"Shit," Karly mutters from the driver's seat. She starts tapping at the GPS on the dash. "Did I miss a turn somewhere?"

The road markings on the map have disappeared from the screen. Now, our little blue dot seems to be traveling through nothing but vast green space.

I reach over to the display and zoom out. "I don't think so. Maybe the GPS just lost signal or something."

Karly glances at me and crinkles her petite nose. "Oh, that's reassuring," she says with a half laugh.

We came off the highway about an hour ago, and we've been winding through a forest of firs ever since. The sky is steel gray, and tall shadows bend along the narrow snaking road. It's super quiet out here, apart from the occasional RV heading in the opposite direction.

Karly glances at me again and purses her rosebud lips. "What should I do? Should I just keep going?" She sits taller, trying to see farther along the zigzagging road. She suddenly looks tiny behind the chunky steering wheel.

I tap on the map display again. "I guess," I answer, frowning at the screen. "Noah said the place is off-grid, right? Maybe some of these roads just aren't recognized." Another soda bottle rolls against my foot.

Piper leans into the front, propping an arm on each of our seats. Her phone is still in her hand, but she's stopped filming. "What's going on? Are we lost? Do not tell me we're lost. I can't deal with that kind of energy."

Karly keeps her focus trained on the road, but her brow furrows and her fingers tighten around the wheel.

"I think it's okay," I tell Piper. "We're heading in the right direction. We'll just have to keep going until we see some road signs."

"Okay, good," Piper breathes. "We cannot get lost out here. Seriously." She curls her lip at the towering trees that line the road. Then, she brightens, placing her hand on my shoulder. "So, Eva," she says, her perfect smile gleaming and red lips bold against her pale skin. She angles her camera toward me and bats her long lashes. "Tell me everything," she says in a singsong voice. "Are you into anyone from school?"

I stiffen at the question. "No comment."

"Are you dating?" she presses.

"No comment." I try to avoid the path of the camera. Unsuccessfully.

Piper pouts her full lips and tilts her head in what I assume is sympathy. "But what about Miles? You two were always together."

I grit my teeth on impulse.

"*Piper*," Karly says, her focus still fixed on the road as she navigates the hairpin bends.

"What?" Her blue-gray eyes pale in the weak sunlight, darting between Karly and me.

"Stop." Karly sweeps aside some of her bangs. "You're in everyone's business, it's too much."

Piper's fingers slip away from my shoulder. "Eva doesn't care, we're bonding. She and Miles were always together, so I was just wondering." She smiles sweetly at me.

I eye the camera lens suspiciously. "Miles and I are just friends," I say to Piper. "We've always been just friends. Nothing more."

"Okay." She falls back into her seat. "Never mind, then."

My gaze wanders back to the winding road, and we fall silent for the first time in a while. That tends to happen whenever Miles is mentioned lately.

But it doesn't last long because Piper turns her questioning to Alice. "How about you, babe?" she asks. "Are you seeing anyone at the moment?"

I watch Alice's response in the mirror. She smiles, but her discomfort is palpable, and I know that it isn't just Piper's nosiness that's getting to her—this isn't the kind of thing that Alice likes to talk to anyone about, including me. She's just private that way. "Nope," she says. "Not right now."

Piper threads her arm through Alice's. "Aw. But you're so pretty, though."

Alice shifts in her seat. "Oh. Thanks."

"Wait," Piper says suddenly, her gaze jumping back to me. "We need to find you girls someone on this trip. All of you." Her hand is back on my shoulder. "I'll make it my mission."

I twist around to face her and muster a noncommittal noise, hoping that's enough to respectfully decline any matchmaking attempts orchestrated by Piper Meyers. Her dating life is a roller coaster that I have zero intention of emulating.

She squints in my direction. "Oh, and in case you were thinking about it," she adds, "do not go there with Danny." She holds my gaze and shakes her head remorsefully. "I know you guys are friends with him and all," she says, looking between Alice and I, "but trust me, you do not want to cross that line. He's not boyfriend material. Total nightmare."

Alice clears her throat. "You and Javier seem good, though," she says, clearly reaching for something positive to steer the conversation along. Neither of us feel comfortable when Piper criticizes Danny. Unfortunately, Piper rarely seems to pick up on our tense expressions or diversion attempts.

She toys with her hoop earring. "For real, I know. Javier is so attentive and considerate. My love languages are *words of affirmation* and *quality time*, so he and I are so much better than Danny and I ever were." She exaggerates a shudder.

"Yeah," I agree, breathing out a laugh. Danny kept most of their turbulent relationship private, but I still caught glimpses of the drama unfolding on Piper's social media accounts. Tearful rants only to be deleted an hour later and replaced with cryptic memes like *know your worth* and *let go of that which does not serve you*. Miles, Alice, and I did our best to be supportive of Danny while he and Piper were on-again, off-again for months, until finally Piper and Javier became the new thing, and Danny was out.

Until they started *talking* again, and we somehow ended up on a group trip to Oregon.

Piper's phone pings from the back seat. "Oh, it's Javier," she says, reading from the screen. "See how we are so in sync? I was literally just talking about him."

"What did he say?" Karly asks.

"Just that the guys are stopping for gas." She looks up from her phone. "Javi says there's a truck stop coming up. We should meet them there."

Karly glances at the digital map on the dash, then gives way to a flustered sigh. "Okay. Did he say where, exactly?" The markings are still MIA from the display.

"No." Piper starts typing back as she talks. "But it's all one road, right? We'll get to it eventually. Just keep going."

A shadow falls over the car as a cloud passes the sun. It makes me shiver a little. I glance at the road map again as we head deeper and deeper into nothing.

PIPER

Hi, besties! It's Piper, filming live from the back seat of Karly's car! We're nearly five hours into our road trip, kinda lost, but all is good, loves.

Here's Karly in the driver's seat. She's such a trooper. As you can see, Eva called shotgun ahead of me. Bitch. Just kidding, I love her, really! And Alice and I owning the back seat. Say hi, Alice!

Guys, please go follow Alice. I'll mention her @ in the comments. We're totally bonding on this trip, and I've seen her IG. She posts the most stunning pictures. She's an artist and creates these beautiful, almost cinematic drawings inspired by her roots in Botswana. She's created this piece for World Wetlands Day, really spotlighting environmental conservation across the country. And I just… No words. Extreme talent. As you guys know, I suck at art. I don't even enjoy it, drawing and that kind of thing. For real, if I could have the work done for me, I'd totally do it. Oh, shit. I probably shouldn't say that because there was this huge cheating thing that happened at our school and our friend got expelled. It was a whole drama, and everyone is just cringing. Major secondhand embarrassment. It's giving me anxiety just thinking about it. So, to be clear, I am not advocating cheating, you guys. That stuff always comes out, anyway.

Okay, I'm going to go because everyone's hating on me right now! They think I talk too much…and they're right!

Love you guys. Kiss, kiss.

EVA

We keep following the lost road until we see a signpost for Bobby's Roadside Diner. Behind a row of gas pumps, there's a mini market with a simple restaurant attached. Karly slows the car and pulls into one of the empty parking bays.

The Demarcos' black Ford is already here. The cargo bed is loaded with surfboards and bags, all held down with ropes and straps. Immediately, I spot Colton leaning against the truck as he fills up the gas tank, his ball cap shading his eyes. He glances our way and lifts his hand in a greeting. On the other side of the truck, Noah has his head down, securing the bags in the back. When Karly cuts the engine, he glances up and then crosses the paved lot toward us. His sandy blond curls move in the breeze.

He stops at the Prius and leans against Karly's open window. His lips twitch with a smile. "Hey."

"Hey," Karly says.

There's been times where I've wondered if Noah and Karly are low-key into each other, judging by the way they talk quietly at the back of class or swap secret looks when they think no one's watching.

I smile to myself at the thought. Noah seems like a good guy; he gives off super laid-back surfer vibes—contradicting the fact that he comes from an extremely driven family of academics. Miles once mourned for an entire week when he found out that Noah's older sister, Samantha, had a GPA one point higher than his, taking the school record. It was a whole thing. Fortunately, *Noah's* grades were never a threat to Miles's ranking in our class—Miles's words, not mine. Karly is a little more put-together than Noah, and she doesn't strike me as being particularly outdoorsy in the way that he is, but she's fun and bubbly. I could see them together.

"You made it, then," Noah says. His sweatshirt sleeves are pushed up to the elbows, and he rests his tanned and muscular forearms on the frame.

Karly tilts her sunglasses down and peers at him over the rim. "Yeah. How much longer until we get to your uncle's place? These roads are intense."

"It isn't far from here," he says, his blue-gray eyes moving between all of us. "Maybe an hour. Are you guys doing okay?"

Piper leans forward, wedging herself between the two front seats. "Oh, we're fine," she says, batting her long eyelashes. "Aren't we, ladies?" She taps my shoulder. "We've just been talking *all* about you, Noah."

His neck flushes red, and Piper laughs. I'm pretty sure I'm blushing, too, from the suggestion in her tone.

"She's kidding," I assure him, and Piper giggles again.

"Where's Javier?" Piper asks.

"He's gone inside to get a table." Noah nods toward the diner across the lot.

"Oh, nice of him to wait for his girlfriend," Piper says, rolling her eyes. Then she drums her manicured nails on Karly's arm. "Will you buy me an iced coffee, K? You're richer than I am." She swats Karly's arm before hopping out of the car and sidling past Noah. Karly gets out after her and they head toward Bobby's Diner, their arms linked, and their shoes clicking fast on the tarmac as they make their way toward the entrance.

Noah raps on the hood of the car before trailing after them. Before I get out, though, I swivel around to face Alice. "Are you surviving?"

She gives me a too-bright smile. "Yeah," she says. "Totally fine. You?"

I squint one eye. "Are you sure you're okay?"

"Yes, Eva. I'm actually having a good time."

My eyebrows knit. "Really?"

"Yes! Aside from the occasional awkward conversation, I'm having fun. Aren't you?"

"I guess," I say slowly. "But it's just that I know how camera shy you are and…"

"I'm getting used to it," she says with a wave of her hand. Then her eyes light up. "Piper's been so complimentary about my art, and she says she'll share some of my pieces on her page. That's huge exposure—she's got a ton of followers." She claps her hands, colorful bracelets jangling on her wrists. "Yay."

"Yay," I agree.

"Piper's the sweetest person."

"Oh-kay." I lower my voice. "Blink twice if you're wearing a wire."

She laughs and unbuckles her seat belt. Leaving it at that, she climbs out of the car.

"Okay, then," I say to myself. I step out onto the pavement, and the Prius locks with a jaunty beep before Karly, Piper, and Noah disappear into the diner with Alice trotting behind.

Colton makes his way over to me as I cross the lot. He smiles as he intercepts my path, but the expression is a little uncertain, like he's wondering if I *want* him to walk with me.

"Hey, Eva," he says. "How's it going?"

He's several inches taller than me, and broader than I remember—I guess he's grown a lot since our days of elementary school parties. In the hazy sunlight, his eyes are a deep ocean green, a shade darker than Danny's, and there's a smattering of freckles beneath his lower lashes.

Colton and Danny share a lot of the same features, the dimpled smiles, straight teeth, and cowlicks in their wavy brown hair. They're both around six feet tall, but Colton's a little more athletic-looking with a deep tan even in the winter. A product of their Italian heritage.

It's funny. Even though Danny's more studious, I've always thought of Colton as the more levelheaded and practical of the two. Sometimes Colton seems like he's carrying the world, and Danny's just coasting through it with his head in the clouds.

"All good," I answer. "You?" My cheeks suddenly feel hot. To my shame, I often find myself blushing when I'm one-on-one with Colton.

"Five-hour car ride with Danny and Javier." He presses his lips together and raises his eyebrows. "Fun."

I laugh. "Yeah, I can imagine."

He takes off his ball cap and runs a hand through his tousled brown hair. "Wanna swap cars?" He's got a cute half smile going on, and I can't help but smile back.

"No, thanks," I say. "Anyway, we've got Piper in ours, so we're expected to join in with her Instagram Lives. I'd wager that's more painful than the whole Danny-dated-Javier's-girlfriend awkward-ness."

He holds up his hands. "Alright. You win."

We start toward the diner entrance, and in the light breeze I catch a rush of the sports spray that he wears.

"So…" I start twisting the strap on my messenger bag, fold-ing it back and forth. My eyes travel over him as we walk. "Are you still working at Summits?"

He grins, and a dimple hollows his left cheek. "Yeah, week-nights and Saturdays. I haven't seen you in there in a while."

Colton works at the mountain and water sports store down-town. They sell tons of outdoor equipment and have a coffee shop and clay rock-climbing wall at the back. Whenever I go in with my parents, my dad always makes a point of talking to Colton. Colton shakes his hand, and Dad's eyes crinkle with a smile as they discuss the latest stock. Mom and Dad always ask Colton how his mom is doing, and Colton always has the same response—*fine*—then he moves the conversation along.

"Hey, tell your dad we've got that roller power unit he was looking for a couple of weeks back," he says. "If he still wants it, I can hold it for him."

"Okay, thanks. I'll let him know."

"Tell him I said hi, too. Your mom as well."

"I will." I know my parents like Colton and Danny. The boys were always firm favorites at my birthday parties—probably because they were the only kids who'd help load the dishwasher or listen intently to my parents' long-winded stories. They'd always stay later than everyone else, too. Sometimes, I got the feeling they didn't want to go home. I remember one time, after my tenth birthday bowling party, it got pretty late and their mom still hadn't shown, so my dad gave them a ride home. But when Dad got back to our house, I saw his 4X4 pull up in the driveway with the boys still in the back seat.

I never directly asked my dad why he didn't drop them off at their own house that night, but I overheard him talking to my mom in the kitchen. "…I couldn't just leave them," he'd muttered. "…Anna must be working late. I tried calling her." I didn't hear my mom's response, I just crept quietly back to the den where the boys were flicking through movies on Netflix. Mom came into the room a few minutes later with a tray of hot cocoas and a huge bucket of popcorn for us to share. Her eyes looked a little glassy behind her overly cheerful smile.

Colton's voice jolts me from the memory. "I'm glad Danny managed to convince you guys to join us this weekend."

I gather myself quickly. "Yeah. Me, too. It was Piper's idea, actually."

His smile turns strained. "Yeah, I heard. I didn't know she and Danny had been talking again."

"Neither did I until a couple of weeks ago."

We reach the entrance to the diner, and Colton holds the door open for me to duck through.

The restaurant is pretty quiet, apart from the clanging of plates and an old-fashioned stereo playing faintly in the background. A long counter runs along the back wall with a couple of older men seated on stools, sipping coffees or polishing off plates of food. Along the front window, there are some tired-looking booths with a view of the parking lot. Our group has gathered in the booth farthest from the door. Danny and Miles are together on one side with Miles's slender frame and blond hair just visible behind Danny. They're kind of hard to miss, actually. Miles is wearing a fluorescent yellow T-shirt with the word *MARVEL* printed across his narrow chest, and Danny is in a psychedelic sweatshirt that reads "A long time ago, in a galaxy far, far away…"

On the other side of the table, I find Alice seated closest to the window, next to Noah, Karly, Piper, and Javier. Piper is perched on Javier's lap with her arm locked around his neck, and Javier is holding court with a wide smile and one hand knotted through his grown-out black curls. Their laughter travels across the diner.

While Colton heads toward them, I scan the restaurant for the bathroom sign. As I start for the opposite end of the diner, my phone buzzes with a text message from Piper.

Do you know?

I frown at the screen and look back toward the booth. Piper's still on Javier's lap, her fingers tangled in his hair. She raises an eyebrow at me before carrying on with her conversation. The sound of her laughter floats across the diner over the clang of plates and drone of voices.

I type back. What??

I see her look at her phone, and then type. Staring at my screen and the little flashing ellipses, I wait for a second.

A moment later, my message alert pings again.

Nothing. Don't worry.

COLTON

Danny keeps tapping on the table. He's on his second coffee, focused on pouring the sugar dispenser and watching the granules sink into the drink.

We're all crammed into one booth. My shoulder keeps knocking Danny's because I'm trying too hard not to invade Eva's space, and Danny can't give me room because Miles is squeezed in on his other side, next to the window. Miles has been staring out into the parking lot for a while, only talking when someone tries to pull him into the conversation.

Next to me, Eva stirs her coffee. It's one of those milky, frothy ones that come in a tall glass. She chews on the end of the wooden stirrer, listening to Piper talk.

"Where are you going to college, Eva?" Piper asks. She's on Javier's lap, and his head is rested against her shoulder.

Eva shifts in her seat. Her gaze flickers to Miles, but his eyes stay trained on the parking lot beyond the window. "I don't know," she says. "I haven't heard back from my schools yet."

Opposite us, Karly takes a small sip of soda. "What is that you want to major in?" she asks Eva.

"Wait," Piper interrupts, raising her hands. "I know this. It's chemistry or something boring like that, isn't it?"

"Marine biology," Eva corrects.

I already knew what her answer would be. She used to talk about it back when we were kids. Her eyes would shine whenever she'd talk about legendary sea creatures or ocean depths that hadn't been explored. A smile tugs at my mouth, because I like that she's still her, still going after her dream.

Piper's attention moves to Danny. "You're staying in Seattle, right?"

"Yeah. They've got a good computer science program." He keeps messing with the sugar pourer, tipping the grains from side to side. "And if I stay local, I can live at home. College dorms *cost*."

"Sometimes the frat houses are cheaper than dorms," Eva points out. "Maybe you could join a fraternity."

He snorts at the suggestion. "Yeah, good one, Eva. Can you really see me in a fraternity?"

She crinkles her nose. "Okay, fair point. You're not really a team player."

Across the table, Alice raises an index finger. "Unless it involves gaming and a bunch of virtual teammates hidden behind elaborate screen names, right?"

Danny grins. "Hell yeah."

"I don't get it when people complain about not having money," Piper says, rolling her eyes. "No shade to you, Danny," she adds, gesturing toward him. "Just that my friend Macie says it all the time. Like it's a valid reason not to hang out. I mean, go get a weekend job or something. Figure it out."

I frown and my attention wanders to Javier. A couple of months ago, back when they were just friends, he would have called her out on a statement like that. But he stays quiet. He never disagrees with her. Never says how he really feels because he's too afraid of losing her.

"It's such a weak excuse," Piper says with a groan. "I can't. Some people are just always with the self-pity. Like, come on."

Danny's arm twitches against mine.

I glance at him, and his jaw clenches as he looks down at the table. I know Danny better than I know anyone. I know Danny better than anyone knows him. And I know that comment was meant for him.

So, I jump in. "What don't you get about it?" I ask Piper.

She looks at me and her dark eyebrows pull together. "What?"

I hold her stare. "You said you don't get it, but if someone doesn't have money to hang out, they can't hang out."

She blinks, then breathes out a tight laugh. "I think you've missed the point, Colton. All I'm saying is that my friend Macie tells me this all the time, and it sounds like an excuse. You can have a perfectly good time without spending money." She narrows her eyes. "You must have misunderstood my meaning."

I press my lips together and shrug. Piper's gaze flickers to Danny, and she raises an eyebrow, like she's saying, *See?* Proving some point she has about me. Danny clears his throat.

The table goes quiet for a second.

"Anyway," Piper carries on, drawing out the word, "I told Macie she should come hang out with Javier and me, but I guess she doesn't want to be a third wheel, and I just feel so bad for her. She literally never comes out."

I lean back in the booth seat when the conversation starts up again with Karly nodding along and Alice making sympathetic noises. Noah gives me a look from across the table, something close to a grin. He covers it quickly, though.

"Do you want this?"

Eva's voice draws my attention to her. She's looking at me, offering some of her candy bar. She tucks a strand of hair behind her ear; it's the same golden brown shade as her eyes.

"Uh, yeah." I stumble over my words. "You don't want it?"

"No, I do. But I'm sharing." She smiles in a way that makes her nose crease. It makes me smile back.

She passes the candy bar to me, and our fingers brush. Her hands are small, soft, and it crosses my mind how rough my skin must seem to her. Too many years of salt water and cold weather. "Thanks, Evie."

She exhales, just a light breath. "Colton," she says, squinting at me, "no one's called me Evie since the sixth grade."

"Oh." My lips twitch. "Sorry."

She shades her eyes with her fingers. "Ugh. Middle school flashbacks."

An easy laugh escapes me, and I sense Danny's eyes on me. He probably hasn't heard me laugh like that in a while. I haven't heard me laugh like that in a while.

"Trust me," I say to Eva, "*you* in middle school is nothing to be embarrassed about." I press my palm to my chest. "Remember who you're talking to."

She takes a sip of the milky coffee and her cheeks dimple with a small smile. "Oh, come on," she says. "You were fine, Colton. I was there. You've always been popular." She waves her hand in my direction. "You've got the whole sports-guy thing going on."

"Lucked out with that, right? I don't have anything else going for me." I grin, because I realized a long time ago that it's easier to be self-deprecating, to own my shit, and make the joke before anyone else can.

Eva touches my hand, just lightly with her fingertips. "That's not true," she says. "You have plenty going for you."

She has this look in her eyes. Not the poor-you look that the parents at the school gate give before they talk about us behind our backs. Just I-hear-you. She's always been able to floor me with that look, because I know she's seeing beyond what I'm showing.

On reflex, I slide my hand away. I regret it as soon as I've done it, but it's too late. She's already pulled her hand back, too. The moment has passed.

Then Danny grabs the candy bar from me and takes a bite, switching up the mood. Because he knows *me* better than anyone, too.

"Thanks, Eva," he says, chewing. "What else have you got over there?" She swats him away, kidding around.

Piper's gaze flickers our way. I swear, she falters, just for a second. The expression on her face, I can't figure it out. Jealousy? Frustration that Danny's having a good time without her maybe. She catches my gaze on her, and like a light bulb switched, she jumps back into her conversation with her side of the booth, giggling loudly and playing with her hoop earring that Danny bought her back when they were dating. That one-second pause, though. That look that no one else seemed to notice.

I noticed.

TWO WEEKS EARLIER

"How's Miles?" I bounce the basketball a couple of times before passing it to my brother.

The sun is starting to set now. Danny and I have been at Cooper's Park's basketball court for a couple of hours, just killing time until it gets too dark to play. The sinking sun has turned the grass beyond the chain-link fence gold, and across the park the streetlamps have come on.

"I don't know," Danny mutters, holding the ball still. "He's not talking."

"Oh, man, that sucks." We all saw Miles emptying his locker last week, and his parents leaving the school office looking like the floor was about to collapse from under them.

"Yeah."

"Is he still coming to the beach with us over the break?"

Danny looks down at his scuffed sneakers. "I don't know. Eva thinks she can convince him. She thinks it'll be good for him. But I don't know."

"He should come. You all should." I hesitate for a second. "Hey, I didn't know you'd been talking to Piper again?" It's taken me a full week to ask that question. I swear, I've been building up to it since I first found out.

"Yeah." Danny bounces the basketball in slow thuds, avoiding my stare. Pretending he can't see it. "We're talking."

He aims for the basket, shoots. The ball rebounds off the rim with a clink of metal, and he cusses under his breath. He jogs across the court to retrieve it.

"What have you been talking about?" I ask as he tosses the ball to me. I catch it and hold it at my chest.

"Just, you know." He wipes his forehead with the bottom of his jersey. His hair is damp with sweat, a sign that we've been out here for a while. A sign that neither of us want to go home.

"You know?" I echo, frowning. "What does you know mean?"

He rolls his eyes. "Come on, Colton. It's not a big deal."

I press my tongue against my teeth. "If it's not a big deal, then why won't you tell me what you've been talking about?"

He shrugs. "Just stuff. Life."

"Like about Mom and stuff?"

He shrugs again.

My shoulders tense, and I grip the ball tighter. "You know Piper and Javier are together now. They're getting serious."

"Yeah, I know that." He exhales and shakes his head. "Would you give me some credit, please? I'm not trying to step on anyone's toes. I thought you'd be glad that Piper and I are good again."

I choke out a laugh. "Why would I be glad about that?"

"Because it means we can all hang out, you and your friends, and me and mine. Now that Piper's with Javier, she's going to be around you guys all the time. Makes it easier for everyone if me and her are good."

"Okay," I mutter. I dribble the ball and take my shot. It sinks through the net, and I jog to catch it on the bounce.

"I thought you'd be happy for me," he says from across the court.

I act like I haven't heard him.

He lifts his hands for me to toss him the ball. So I do. Too hard.

He grips it at his chest, eyebrows drawn together. "What was that for?"

I want to tell him that I think he's out of his mind. That this is going to blow up in his face, like it always does. That he and Piper were never good. I want to remind him of all the brutal things she said to him, about him, all around school, all over social media. She dragged him through it, broke his heart, and I can't forget that.

I don't want him *to forget that.*

But I just say sorry and watch him take his shot.

DMEA GROUP CHAT

EVA: What's the vibe in your car? Is it as terrible as you'd imagined, Miles?

MILES: Meh. Danny's annoying me.

EVA: As usual, then.

MILES: It's my cross to bear.

DANNY: HEY. WTF???

MILES: Kidding. Partially. How's your car, E?

EVA: We're doing okay. We have Skittles, so...

ALICE: Lots of Skittles.

MILES: Have you featured in any of Piper's IG stories yet?

EVA: Our very own Alice is the new star.

DANNY: So Piper's being nice to you all?

EVA: Define nice.

ALICE: She is! I really like her. But I've always said that.

DANNY: Yeah, I knew you guys would get along.

MILES: I'm not convinced.

EVA: Piper texted me privately in the diner just saying: Do you know? Am I supposed to know something?

MILES: You're supposed to know many things.

ALICE: Don't ask me. I'm always the last to know everything!

EVA

A narrow road snakes through the forest. Karly's Prius joggles over the bumps, following behind the truck with three surfboards bouncing precariously in the cargo bed. All around us, vibrant green ferns blanket the ground.

After a little while, the forest road opens out into a clearing where a rectangular log-walled building stands alone, flanked by a few evergreens. Beyond, I can see a strip of silver ocean, almost disappearing into the pale sky.

Karly pulls over in the clearing and cuts the engine. "Oh," she says, peering through the windshield at the lodge in front of us. "This must be it."

"Looks like it," I murmur.

The log building is raised on stilts with a wraparound porch sheltered by a sloping roof. An A-frame reception cabin is on one end, leading on to five motel-style rooms all attached.

Everything is wooden, from the planked porch deck to the doors and outer log walls.

I unfasten my seat belt and follow Karly, Piper, and Alice out of the car. The cold air tastes like salt and pine, damp from the marine wind.

Danny, Miles, and Colton are already carrying the surfboards to the lodge, climbing the wooden steps that lead to the deck. Lagging behind a little, Miles catches my gaze and exaggerates a grimace, gesturing to whoever's surfboard he's been landed with.

I smile back at him as I follow the girls to the truck, where Javier and Noah are busy unloading the backpacks from the back.

"Hey," Piper sings. She rises to her tiptoes and kisses Javier's cheek.

Tall and lanky, he stoops and slings a lean arm around her shoulders, trapping down her silky black hair, then he looks between us with a toothy smile. "Look at this, right? What do you think?" he asks us with wide-eyed enthusiasm.

Piper wrinkles her delicate nose.

But Javier doesn't seem to notice her reaction; he's still gazing at the lodge in awe, his tie-dye T-shirt fluttering in the breeze. The long wraparound deck hangs over a golden beach with a view to the silver ocean, where monoliths rise from the water and rocky sea caves fringe the shoreline.

Alice is wearing the same awed expression as Javier. I'm pretty sure it's mirrored on my face, too. "Noah," Alice says, blinking at him in disbelief. "Your uncle owns this whole place?"

Noah pauses midway through unbuckling a strap in the flatbed. "Yeah," he says, raking a hand through his sun-bleached curls. "He bought it at foreclosure last year. It came with the land, too. But the lodge needs a ton of work done on it before he can get it to code, so he hasn't been able to officially open to guests yet. Not paying ones, anyway," he adds with a quick grin.

I glance over my shoulder at the log building, and the scattering of trees surrounding it. It's completely secluded. Completely peaceful with only the *shh*-ing sound of the tide and the occasional cry of a gull. Colton, Miles, and Danny have already disappeared into the A-frame cabin. The door is still ajar, softly batting in the wind.

"My uncle offers it out to the family when he isn't using it," Noah adds. "The catch is, he lets us stay on the basis that we'll do a couple of odd jobs for him while we're here."

Piper sucks in a breath.

"Nothing big," Noah assures her. "Just like painting, cleaning, and there are a couple of things that need fixing."

She folds her arms. "Okay, just FYI, I'm not doing any work while I'm here. I'm on vacation."

"Babe." Javier's smile looks uncomfortable.

"What?" Piper blinks back at him. "No one said anything about manual labor. Like, it took a lot to convince my parents to let me come here unsupervised, and I'm not spending my time cleaning and painting." She glances at Karly and rolls her eyes, mouthing, "*What the eff?*"

Noah's gaze moves to Javier, and Javier shrugs.

"Okay," Noah says tightly. "No worries."

"We can help," Alice says, pointing between the two of us.

He gives us a nod. "Thanks. We're just going to keep working on some stuff we started last time. We came out here a few months back, Javier, Colton, Danny, and me." He pauses and takes a deep breath of ocean air. "I love it out here. This place was built before regulations so it's the only property in the area set this close to the beach."

"Man." Javier shakes his head, and the breeze fluffs his dark hair. "Your uncle's going to be earning big when he can rent this out. I need some tips—your family knows how to get rich," he says with a booming laugh.

Noah's laughter sounds a little tense, and his neck flushes red. He returns his attention to the straps binding the luggage.

Piper leans into Javier, placing a manicured hand on his chest. "So, this is it?" she asks. "It's just this?" She glances at Karly again, who hugs her arms around herself, her long red hair stirring in the wind.

"Yup." Noah heaves a backpack out of the cargo bed and drops it onto the ground with a thump. "This is it."

"Oh."

Karly checks her phone, lifting it a little higher. "There's hardly any cell service," she mutters.

I glance at Alice, and she winces.

"Yeah, it's spotty," Noah says.

Piper checks her phone, too. "They have Wi-Fi here, though?"

Noah breathes out a laugh. "Piper. My uncle hasn't even opened the place yet. You really think he's installing Wi-Fi just for us?"

She rubs her temples, and Javier tightens his hold around her, moving his big hand up and down her arm. "Relax," he says, squeezing her shoulder. "You're going to love it."

She looks like she's forcing a smile. "Of course. I was just expecting more."

I swap another glance with Alice while Noah and Javier stare blankly at Piper.

"No, I mean, it's fine," she says, waving her hand. "It's cute, and whatever. Just, I thought we were going to be in a town with shops and bars?" She raises the last word into a question, looking at Noah for an answer.

He returns his attention to the truck, untangling another backpack from the ties. "No, I told you," he says, loosening the rope. "It's off-grid."

Piper bares her teeth into a smile. "Yeah, but when you said *off-grid*, I didn't think you meant it literally. I thought we were in a resort."

"We are," he says. "This is it."

The already strained smile somehow gets even tighter. "Okay." She pauses and shivers. "It's a little cold out here, isn't it?"

As if on cue, my hair is spiraled by the same wind that howls through the trees and drives the ocean to crash against the shore. There's something opaque about the sky, like it's closing in on us.

"It'll be warmer inside," Noah says, heaving the last bag from the cargo bed and shrugging it onto his broad shoulder. "We can light the fire. Let's go."

Piper taps her fingernail on her teeth and casts another glance at Karly, who stiffly unsticks her boot heel from the mud.

In convoy, we all follow Noah up the wooden porch steps.

As the others head inside, I catch Piper's sleeve on the threshold. She pauses, glancing between me and the cabin with its scuffed wood floor and open-concept lounge. We stay on the planked deck for a moment, letting the others go ahead. Wind whistles through the tall wooden structure.

This is the first time I've been alone with Piper since the diner, and I've been bursting with questions. "What was that message about?" I ask under my breath. "What do you think I know?"

She looks at me for a second, long dark lashes framing bright blue eyes. "Oh, nothing." She smiles sweetly. Too sweetly.

Then her eyes drift back to the cabin. Through the open door, her gaze lands on Colton where he's leaning against the sofa, talking to Miles and Danny. She smiles at me again before skipping into the cabin.

SIX MONTHS EARLIER

"What's going on with Colton?" Miles doesn't look at me when he asks the question. His eyes stay glued to his project on the computer in Mr. Harris's classroom. His slender fingers tap fast on the ancient keyboard.

I lift my soda and balance the straw between my lips. "What do you mean?"

"Are you going to tell him you're into him?"

I almost choke on my drink. "Excuse me?"

"What?" He tears his eyes away from the computer screen just long enough to frown at me. "Are you denying it?"

I squirm at the question. Most of the class have gone to lunch now. But Karly, Noah, and Danny are still at their table across the room, working on their group project. They're laughing, tossing balled-up paper at each other. They're not paying attention to us. But still, a little discretion would be nice. If Danny overhears, he'll undoubtedly hold this over me for all eternity. And if, by some miracle, he didn't tell

Colton, then Noah certainly would. Plus, I could do without Karly asking me a ton of questions, like when did I know? What am I going to wear when we hook up? Or worse, offering to talk to him for me.

I shudder at the thought.

Miles has returned to his report now, saving it to the online portal. The loading icon flashes on the screen.

"I don't think about Colton like that," I whisper, though even I can hear how unconvincing it sounds. "And please don't go broadcasting this."

Miles jiggles the mouse as he tries to refresh the page. "What, that you don't like him?"

"No, that I do."

He glances at me and furrows his brow. "I thought you said you didn't."

I take another sip of soda, holding his stare.

He directs his pen at me. "You know I have limited patience for this kind of conversation."

I roll my eyes.

Miles turns his attention back to the screen and takes a sharp breath. "What the hell?" he says, and I follow his gaze. The portal page has frozen with an error message. He slaps his hands to his temples, dragging his fingers through pale blond hair. "You have got to be kidding me," he mutters. He hits the refresh button, and suddenly the entire page disappears.

"Oh, no." I place my soda on the table and lean closer to the computer screen. "Did you lose your project?"

He taps fast on the keypad. "I don't know," he murmurs distractedly. "I think I just deleted it from the network." His chair scrapes as he stands abruptly, then he slings his backpack over his shoulder and strides across the room.

He bypasses Danny's table, and for a second, I think he's going to walk right out. So I grab my bag and follow. But Miles doesn't head out to lunch, he stops at Mr. Harris's desk and slides into the teacher's chair.

I watch uncomfortably as he pops open Mr. Harris's laptop and enters a password at superfast speed.

"Uh, Miles." I prod his arm. "I don't think you're allowed to log in to a teacher's personal account."

He waves his hand. "It's fine. I've got to log on as admin so I can retrieve a deleted file. Simon won't mind."

"Uh, I don't think you're supposed to call him by his first name, either."

He doesn't respond.

I shift from left to right, trying to ignore the blatant security breach going on in front of me, pretending to be fascinated by a peeling wall display instead. I knew Miles had the admin password so that he can work on the yearbook but playing around on Mr. Harris's personal computer seems like a step too far.

"Okay," he says with a relieved breath. "I found it, it's fine. Just saving to the portal, and then we are…done." He exits the web page. "Oh," he says slowly.

I hold my gaze on him. "What?"

"Oh." He closes the laptop with a thump. "I think I saw something I wasn't supposed to see."

"What did you see?"

"Don't ask," he says. "Let's just go."

My brow knits, and he shakes his head. He grabs his backpack and is out of the door so fast that I practically have to run to catch up with him.

EVA

By the time I step into the cabin, Piper's already set to work staging the space for pictures, angling her phone to get the best shot of the rustic room. Looking around, I close the door behind me, trapping the cold air outside.

Two tan leather couches face each other on either side of a log fireplace. Above the hearth, there's a thick oak ledge with an arrangement of cylinder candles with wax bleeding down their sides. The entire room is a pallet of browns and oranges, knotty pine walls and woven rugs, and there's a huge pair of antlers mounted on the wall above the fireplace.

Across the lounge area, there's a kitchenette with pine cabinets that look like they date back a few decades, and tall windows overlooking the sloping beach below. A patio door leads out onto the back deck.

Miles crosses the room to join me, smoothing down some of his neat hair. "Okay," he says slowly, standing beside me and folding his arms. "I think I can get behind this. It's giving me early pioneer meets Malibu beach house." He creates a frame with his thumbs and forefingers, squinting one eye as he looks through the square shape.

"I get that," I agree with a nod.

"But I'm not a fan of…" He waves in the direction of the antlers mounted above the fireplace.

I wrinkle my nose and turn to him. "Okay, so, I've checked the tide chart, we're a little before low tide. I've done my research and the rock pools around here will be worth exploring."

He narrows his eyes. "I'm not going into the water. I don't do that."

"Just tide pooling."

"Shallow pools," he says, raising his palm. "Nothing that'll get my jeans wet."

"Shallow pools," I concede. "Deal."

"Deal," he echoes.

We shake on it and head for the patio door. With the exception of Colton, who's busy waxing his surfboard in the middle of the open room, and Noah, who's systematically checking through the kitchen cabinets, everyone else is already out on the back deck. Miles and I stop in the kitchen area to wait for Noah. As he finishes unloading the last of our supplies into an unused cabinet, my eyes are drawn to the tall windows, and the beach gently inclining down to the water, where white-capped waves are crashing against the shore.

Noah notices my wandering gaze and grins. "What do you think? It's good, right?"

"It's amazing," I breathe. "Thanks so much for inviting

us." I glance at Miles and frown. "Actually, thanks so much for not saying no when Danny invited us."

"No problem. There's plenty of space. I'm glad you guys came."

"Your uncle is a lucky guy," Miles adds.

"Yeah, he's living the dream." Noah closes the cupboard, and we head for the clear patio door. He pauses, his eyes lost on the beach beyond the glass. "Buying and renovating properties, total freedom to make his own rules. Sometimes I think about blowing off college and going for a life like this instead." He stops short and glances at Miles.

Miles's ears turn pink. "Please," he says with a tight smile. "You don't have to say that for my benefit. You got into your school of choice, *that's* living the dream."

"I wasn't…" Noah looks down at his sneakers. "Sorry. I didn't mean it like that."

"It's fine." Miles straightens his thin shoulders before stepping out onto the blustery deck. He doesn't hold the patio door for us, and it slides shut behind him.

Noah turns to me and raps his fist on his forehead. "I didn't mean it like that," he says with a wince. "I was just talking about my uncle. *Shit.* I shouldn't have said that."

"Don't worry," I tell him, quietly. "Miles is just hypersensitive about everything right now. Don't take it personally."

"Yeah," he murmurs. "He's not doing so good, huh?"

"I don't know, he's not really talking. But he'll be okay," I say, probably more for myself than for Noah. I return my attention to the clear glass door. Miles has joined Danny, and they're forging a path down some uneven stone steps descending to the sand. Karly, Piper, Alice, and Javier are already on the beach, their hair whipping back and forth with the wind.

I watch Danny bolt across the sand, kicking up grains behind him. He dives into the shallows, fully clothed, while Miles stands rigidly on the shoreline, arms folded tightly.

The sound of laughter echoes across the bay, sounding almost melancholy in the desolation of the cove.

And I realize with a strange chill, there's no one here but us.

COLTON

Noah leaves through the back door, stepping out onto the deck. But Eva hesitates before she follows him. She turns and looks at me. "Are you coming with us, Colton?"

Everyone else has gone down to the beach. It's just us now.

"I'll catch up to you," I tell her. "I just need a couple more minutes."

"Okay." Then her smile changes, turning almost shy, and she adds, "Do you think I could have a go on your board sometime this trip?"

"Sure. You can take it right now." Her eyebrows raise, and I've even taken myself by surprise with the offer. But I stand and carry the surfboard to her.

"Thanks, Colton." Her eyes light up in the best way as she takes the board from me. Handing it over, just for that look, was worth it. "That's so nice of you," she says. "I promise I won't damage it."

"It's alright. I trust you, Eva." Then I joke, "Just don't let Danny near it. He breaks everything."

She grins and crosses her heart with her index finger, and then she leaves. The door rattles shut behind her.

Alone in the cabin, I grab the keys from the main door and head back out onto the front deck. A cool salty breeze ripples my T-shirt.

I stuff my hands into my jacket pockets and head for the farthest door along the outer corridor. Just like the communal cabin, the bedrooms are log-walled with exposed floorboards and cloth lampshades. None of them have much furniture—two single beds in each with a tired shower room attached. Some of the lights flicker, and some don't work at all.

I unlock the door marked 5 and drop my bag onto one of the twin beds, then I cross the room and lean against the dusty window ledge. The others are all out on the beach. I can hear them shouting, calling to each other.

Tuning out the sound, I take my phone from my pocket and pull up a new message box. I'm sorry about what I said yesterday, I type. I didn't mean it.

I hit Send. My one wavering service bar blinks.

Message Delivery Failed.

I toss my phone onto the bed and take a seat on the edge of the mattress. Staring at the pine wall, I lock my hands in front of me.

The echoes of cries and shouts haunt the cove.

I glance at the window, just in case. But they're all okay; they're having fun. This place can be dangerous, though. Behind the picture-perfect veneer, it's got some sharp teeth.

PIPER

ALBUM: SAVED VIDEOS

Hey, besties! It's Piper. Disclaimer, I'm filming this video in real time, but who knows when I'll be able to post it because the cell service out here is the worst.

But we're finally at the accommodations and I just wanted to give you a quick room tour.

So, right now I'm out on the deck, and when I tell you it is freezing out here. Oh, my god. I am not kidding, my hands are completely numb right now, guys.

This is the communal room. Cute fireplace, cozy couches, and gorgeous views from every window. Oh, hang on. Let me just zoom in. I don't know if you can see this, but that's Javier right there, about to go into the water with his board. Go follow him @JavierRamosSurfs.

Okay, so, now we're heading back out onto the deck, and

on to the first room, which Karly and I have claimed. As you can see, they have these cute patchwork comforters and rustic feel throughout, which I am in love with. And let me just show you this. I've brought in some of these little pine cones from outside to decorate the window ledge right here. So cute.

Oh, look at this top. This is Karly's. I'm obsessed with how soft it is, and this silvery gray color is so on trend right now. Karly got this from Candy Blush Boutique, and she actually used my discount code to get it. I'll share my code with you in the comments if you want to shop and get 10 percent off your first order. Super cute clothes, guys. Please do check out their online store.

Okay. I'm going to take you through to some of the other rooms now. Wait, let me just knock to make sure no one's in there changing or anything. Okay, I think we're good. I'm going in.

This is Miles's room, I think. Yeah, that's his backpack. I remember him always scurrying around school with it, and it made him look so tiny in comparison. Bless. As you can see in here, it's similar to my room, but maybe a little smaller.

Next, we have Noah and Javi's room. Zooming in on Noah's surfboard right there—I can tell you, Javier is obsessed with this board, it's basically the best around, apparently. Very nice. And another view to the beach.

Okay, on to Alice and Eva's room. Not much to see here, doesn't look like they've unpacked yet. I'll have a little snoop later, see what clothes they've brought. Though I know it's all going to be pretty basic.

On to the final room. This one's Danny and Colton's. As you can see, a total mess. That's definitely Danny's side, my ex. It does not surprise me. Danny's kind of a mess in general. He's just an all-round weak excuse for a person, be warned.

Just kidding!

Anyway, that's it. I'll be vlogging the whole trip, and hopefully I'll be able to post these, if not in real time, then whenever I'm in a signal-friendly zone. So keep checking for my posts and updates. Seriously, I've got so much content in store for you guys over these next few days, you do not want to miss this. I'm feeling in the mood to share.

Love you guys!

COLTON

"There are loads of rocks over here," I call. "Just watch out, okay?" I'm treading water in the cold current. It's strong, and the waves are capping at about six feet. But Eva doesn't seem fazed. She's straddling my board, hair darkened from the water and ponytail clinging to her shoulder over her swimsuit. I try to act normal, like I'm not hyperaware of her presence. Like she isn't the only thought in my head.

Swimming around the board, I push the nose away from the rocks as she drags her hand through the water.

"I'm going to take this one," she says, looking toward the horizon as the next swell starts to build behind us. I move out of the way, heading for the rocks, something to hold on to against the tide. Eva lies flat on the board and starts to paddle. She gets into position, and I watch as she pops up. The swell carries her for a while and then she disappears into the breaker.

I squint, holding my breath as I wait for her to resurface.

The nose of the board comes up, and then I see her. She lifts her hand from the water, waving. The look of exhilaration on her face makes me smile, and I leave the rocks and swim toward her. She's already clinging to the board, grinning as water spills down her face. I hold on to the other side and push the wet hair back from my brow.

"That was so good!" she exclaims, breathlessly. Her eyes are every shade of gold in the weak sunlight.

"Yeah, I saw." My face aches from smiling. I can't help but smile when I'm with her; it's the effect she has on me. "You wanna go again?"

She nods quickly. Treading water, I hold the board steady, and she pulls herself up. I've never shared my board with anyone before. I usually want to be out on it myself, but I like being here, in the water, watching someone else get the same rush I do. Or maybe it's just her that I like.

Another swell starts to build, so I let go of the board. She catches the wave, and it carries her away, disappearing into the rip curl.

When she reappears, she's already back on the board and paddling against the current toward me, still smiling. We both are.

I wait at the rocks as another surge builds, but she lets it pass. The board dips with the motion but she allows the wave to carry on without her, rising into a white-foamed crest closer to the shore.

Then I notice where her attention is. Alice and Piper are on the rock projection at the water's edge, peering into the shadowed mouth of the sea cave with their arms knotted. They edge closer to the hollow in the rock wall, as though they're looking at something inside. Closer. Then Javier jumps out at them, springing from the shadows, and their high-pitched shrieks rebound across the bay.

I tense.

But their laughter follows. They're just messing around. Javier waves seaweed above Piper's head as she tries to cower behind Alice.

Eva's voice pulls me back. "Looks like they're all getting along well."

"Yeah," I call back, and I swim toward her. "Should we go join them?"

"Okay. Do you want to get on?" she asks, sitting upright on the board and shuffling forward to make room for me.

"Yeah?"

She nods, wiping water from her sun-tanned forehead. I pull myself up, and the board rocks. I'm aware of how close we are, our skin touching. She can probably feel my heart beating fast against her shoulder blade.

The board steadies and we start moving with the current, heading toward the shore.

"Thanks for letting me steal your board today," Eva says, and I hear the smile in her voice.

"Anytime. Have you ever been out to Half Moon Bay in Westport?" I ask her, slowly kicking through the water as we drift closer to the rocks.

She shakes her head. "Is that where you go with Javier and Noah?"

"Yeah. There are three surf spots that all face different directions, and the waves get big, it's wild. Before we got our licenses, we used to take a five-hour bus ride to get there and camp out for the weekend. We'd tell our parents that we were staying at each other's houses and all that."

"You never got caught?" she asks.

"*I* didn't. My mom…" I trip over the words. "I don't know, she didn't check up on stuff like that. She probably wouldn't have noticed if I was there or not." My stomach tightens. I don't know why I'm telling her this, but the words keep coming. "She used to skip out for the weekend sometimes, too."

There's a moment, agonizingly long seconds, where she doesn't say anything. My heart starts beating too fast.

Then she speaks. "I'm sorry, Colton," she says softly.

"No, I mean…" I clear my throat. "It's not a big deal."

"Yeah," she says, but the murmur of her voice makes me think she doesn't buy that.

So I move on. "Danny says you're thinking about staying in Seattle for college?"

She goes quiet.

"What's wrong?"

She doesn't respond right away.

The board bobs with the current as we head closer toward the shore and the hollow sea cave at the water's edge, where Alice, Piper, and Javier are posing for photos, their voices lost in the whistle of the wind. The sun is sinking lower in the sky, and it's getting choppier out here. A breath of wind skims the rippling surface.

"I actually got into Boston as well," Eva says at last. "And I really like the sound of their marine biology program. But I'd feel weird accepting a place in Boston now that Miles isn't going to Harvard. I'd feel like I'm betraying him somehow. I haven't told him yet, actually. I haven't told anyone."

I watch her trace her fingers over the water, drops glistening on her skin. "You've got to do what's right for you. Miles wouldn't blame you for that. You've worked hard, and you deserve that place, if you want it."

She heaves a sigh. "Maybe. What about you?" she asks, pushing the conversation along and away from her. "Where will you be going?"

I steel myself. "I'm not going to college."

"Oh. Okay."

"Yeah. It's not for me."

She hesitates. "Okay. I didn't know that. I thought you wanted to. I mean, I just assumed, because you always used to talk about majoring in English…"

My teeth clench. "Yeah. I changed my mind." It stirs something in me, the fact that she remembered. She knew.

The current pulls us toward the rocks and the shadowed mouth of the cave.

Eva inclines against me as the board dips with the tide. I take it all in before we reach the others. Here, in this private moment away from everyone else, I like the closeness. I *feel* close to her, not just physically, with her leaning against my chest, her wet hair clinging to *my* skin now, and our breathing quickening at every inadvertent touch. But I feel comfortable. It makes me feel like I can tell her anything. Everything.

But I know that I won't.

ONE YEAR EARLIER

I open the front door with my shoulder, then kick the bottom with my sneaker until the latch clicks shut. It's hot out today, and I can hear the fan oscillating from somewhere inside the house.

My navy Summits work shirt feels heavy and thick. I tug at the collar.

"Colton? Is that you?" *Mom's voice drifts through the single-story house, coming from the kitchen.*

"Yeah," *I call back.* "I'm home. I'm going to go take a shower." *I start through the hallway, but her voice stops me.*

"Colton, would you come in here for a moment, please?"

We've only lived in this house for a couple of years. Just two bed-rooms, one bathroom, and a heap of tired furniture that we got from Goodwill.

I head for the kitchen and stop in the doorway. Around the small foldaway table, Mom and Danny are sitting opposite Eileen and Silas. Eileen smiles up at me from her seat, her aged hands folded around a mug of coffee and her gold wedding band glinting on her ring finger. It wouldn't surprise me if she hasn't taken that ring off in the entire fifty years that they've been married. Silas, wearing his own gold band, stands to shakes my hand. His hazel eyes shine, crinkling around the edges.

He grips my hand for a second longer. "Good to see you, Colton." *His voice is hoarse, and his eyes linger on mine with a mixture of warmth and something else. Something close to guilt.*

I see that look he gives me. I recognize it. I know he feels guilty; he's told me so himself, no matter how many times I brush it off. Or how many times I tell him not to sweat it.

My dad might not have stuck around, *I told Silas once,* but you did.

I've only met my dad a couple of times, back when I was a kid. He's been out of the picture for a while now, in and out of jail. Some-times I want to ask Eileen and Silas about him, what he was like at my age, what he's like now. But we don't talk about him. He's the elephant in every room.

Eileen stands from the table now, too. She hugs me, her fluffy white crown of hair barely reaching my chin. "Why don't you come sit down with us," she says kindly.

So I do. We all sit around the too-small table. Mom, Danny, Eileen, Silas, and me.

"What's going on?" I ask them.

Mom looks at me and smiles, and I feel it. For once, she doesn't look tired, or stressed, or broken. She looks relieved.

Eileen folds her lined hand over Silas's. "We have something important we'd like to discuss with you. Your grandfather and I have thought a lot about this," she says, looking between Danny and me. "You boys are about to go into your final year at high school, and we're so, so proud of how hard you both work."

Silas nods, and his eyes turn glassy. Eileen squeezes his hand.

"We want you to know," she says, "that we have some savings, and we'd like to pay for you both to go to college."

I swear I nearly fall off my seat. I sink forward onto the table, just as Danny leans backward, locking his hands behind his head. He chokes out a laugh.

"What?" I murmur, my eyes jumping between Eileen and Silas. "Are you serious?"

Eileen tilts her head. "I know money's tight," she says, glancing at Mom. "And you're our grandkids. It would be our honor to pay for your education."

Tears start streaming down Mom's face. She's on her feet. They all are; Mom, Eileen, and Silas, hugging and kissing cheeks. In the chair next to me, Danny's eyes are red, and he rubs them with his sleeve.

I clap my hand on his shoulder. "Thank you so much," I man-

age to say. It must be shock, what I'm feeling, because I never imagined this. I never thought it would be possible for me, no matter how many extra shifts I take at Summits. Whatever I earn, I've still got to help Mom with bills and groceries. I hardly ever end the month with anything more than pocket change. Saving up for college was just a pipe dream I once had.

Silas returns to his seat and gives us a shaky smile. "But you boys have gotta work hard and get the grades," he says, trying to sound strict even with a voice filled with pride and emotion. "No slacking off."

"We won't," I promise him. "This mean so much…" I trail off and swallow.

Danny chokes out another sound.

My chest tightens. This is the moment our lives change.

I look at Danny and my mouth tugs into a smile. This is happening for us. It's real. There's no way we can screw this up.

EVA

"Oh, I like those jeans on you." Karly approves my outfit with a nod as I step out of the en suite in my room, still towel-drying my hair. She's sitting cross-legged on the floorboards in front of the full-length mirror nailed to the wall.

Her compliment surprises me for a second. I would have thought my clothes were way too ordinary to ever get Karly's seal of approval. But I guess we've bonded a little since the road trip out here, and we've started treating each other like friends rather than friends-by-association.

Alice is on her bed with the patchwork comforter wrapped over her slender shoulders and her long black braid hanging over the material. Her sketchbook is open on the bed with an abstract drawing of the cove half-finished on the page. At the window, Piper leans against the ledge, framed by the setting sun. She quietly assesses me as I cross the room and drape my towel over the back of an old wicker chair.

"I feel like we should go out tonight," Piper says suddenly, her eyes darting to each of us.

Alice half laughs. "Right. And where would we go?"

"I don't know." Piper fiddles with the pendent on her necklace, rolling it between her thumb and forefinger. "Anywhere! This is supposed to be our spring break, and I'm standing here bored. We need to have some fun."

Alice laughs again, and Piper exaggerates a sigh as she wanders across the room, her eyes trailing over everything, inspecting everything. "But what are we supposed to do, just hang out here all night?"

"Yeah." I drag a brush through my hair and scoop it into a ponytail, smoothing down the damp, light brown ends. "That's kind of the idea."

"We've got food and beers and stuff," Karly adds. Her focus is back on the mirror as she dabs her makeup sponge over her forehead. "We'll have our own party."

"I guess." Piper comes to a stop at my bed and fishes a slinky gray top from the pile of clothes that's accumulated on top of the comforter. "Karls, this is yours, isn't it? You should wear it tonight so I can take photos and tag Candy Blush Boutique."

"I'll wear it tomorrow," Karly says as she drops the sponge back into her makeup bag. "I'm already dressed."

Piper scrunches her nose as she returns the top to the pile. Then, with a few bounding strides, she crosses the room to join Alice on her bed.

"Okay, girls," she says, glancing between us, "just a heads-up, Javi's going to stay in my room tonight, so Karly, you're going to need to crash in here."

Karly's attention shoots to Piper. "Uh, no!"

Piper's face falls. "What? Why?"

"Where do you expect me to sleep? There are only two tiny beds in here and they're both taken!"

Clasping her hands together, Piper bats her sweeping eyelashes. "Please, Karls. Javier and I almost never get time alone, you know that. You can squeeze in with one of the girls, right?" She looks expectantly between Alice and me, and we nod half-heartedly in response. "Or you can sleep with Noah," Piper adds, drumming her fingers together. "Since you and Noah get on *so* well and all." She exaggerates a wink, and Karly dips her gaze. Her cheeks flush.

"It's okay," Alice jumps in. "We can switch rooms, Karly. I'll move my stuff to Miles's room. He's alone, anyway, and there's an extra bed. He might appreciate the company."

Piper makes a shrill sound and one hand flutters to her chest. "I. Am. Shook," she says, extending her fingers wide. "Why did I not see this before? Alice, you and Miles? I am *living* for this!"

Alice rolls her eyes. "We're just friends, Piper."

"That's how it begins."

"Not in this case," Alice says, playing with the end of her braid. "Trust me, it's not a thing."

The disappointment is obvious in Piper's pout. "Okay, so, what are we going to do about you, then?" Her bracelets clunk on her wrist as she prods Alice's arm. "Who can I set you up with, if not Miles?"

"No one." Alice folds her arms around herself. "I don't need to be set up with anyone." She stumbles a little over her words, and I try to catch her gaze.

"Come on," Piper says, practically bouncing. "I need to do something with my time. This can be my new project."

"My love life is fine, thanks," Alice says with a tight smile.

"Ooh, why? Because you've already got something going?" She grabs Alice's arm. "And you didn't tell me? I thought I was your new bestie."

"No, just…" Alice slips her arm free. "No, it's not anyone's business."

Knowing Alice, she'll be squirming at this kind of pressure. "Anyway," I say, changing the subject to help her out, "maybe we can go to town tomorrow—"

"Oh, my god." Piper sits bolt upright and presses a hand to her chest. "Please don't tell me it's Danny."

"No," Alice fumbles for words again. "No. I just…"

"What?"

"I just don't—"

"Oh, my god," Piper cuts her off. "It is Danny, isn't it?"

"*Stop*," Alice snaps, taking all three of us by surprise. "It's none of your business, and I don't have to give you an answer. I don't appreciate being ambushed like this. My business is my business, okay? Not yours."

Piper looks taken aback for a second. I'm pretty sure we all do—Alice included. I've never seen her lose her cool like that, and I can tell from the way she's biting her lip that she didn't like doing it.

"Oh-kay," Piper says, catching Karly's gaze across the room and raising an eyebrow. "Message received." She hops off the bed and brushes a piece of lint from her curve-hugging pants. "Well, I guess I'm going to go find the boys since I'm obviously not welcome here."

"Piper, wait," Alice says, recovering quickly. "I'm sorry. I didn't mean to…"

But Piper's already at the door. "Bye, girlies," she sings as she strides out of the room. The door thumps shut behind her.

FIVE MONTHS EARLIER

When we get to the entrance to the movie theater, Danny and Miles are already there.

"Piper's mad at me," Danny says.

Alice has barely had a chance to drop her car keys into her purse before he springs his announcement on us. She shoots him a sympathetic look as she rummages around her bag for her cell.

"How come?" I ask.

I notice Miles roll his eyes as Danny says, "Because I'm at the movies with you guys, and she says I never go with her."

Alice's attention snaps up. "Oh, no! Danny. Why didn't you invite her to come? Now she's going to hate us."

"She already hates us," Miles interjects dryly.

"No, she doesn't," Danny says as we walk into the carpeted complex. It's busy with groups of people lining up for tickets, and everything smells like hot popcorn and candy. "Anyway, I did invite her. But she can't come on Wednesdays because she does yoga with Karly. I said to her, though, I ain't going to the movies on Saturday night when I can see the same film on a Wednesday for half the price."

I glance around at the queues of people. Wednesdays are always extra crowded because the movie theater runs a two-for-one offer.

"Then," Danny says as we join the line for the confectionaries, "she said I always bail on her because I claim I don't have cash,

which is true, but she says I manage to find money when it's something I want to do."

"Which is also true," Miles points out.

Danny frowns at him. "Partially true."

"Half-true," I add. "Half-price true."

The line moves, and we all shuffle forward a few inches.

"But I basically never go to the movies," Danny reasons. "When was that last time I came with you guys?"

"Sixteen weeks ago," Miles answers.

"So," Danny carries on, "she called it a toxic trait and hung up on me."

Alice's face falls. "Oh, no."

Miles rolls his eyes again, and the line edges forward.

"Yeah." Danny stuffs his hands into his jacket pockets. "Now she's putting me on blast on TikTok and saying we're over. It's going viral." He turns his attention to the menu displayed over the popcorn bar.

"Are you over?" I ask.

He shrugs. "I don't know. Probably not."

Miles catches my gaze, then he clears his throat. "May I speak on behalf of the cohort?"

Danny tears his eyes away from the menu board and curls his lip. "Is the cohort you three?" He thumbs between us.

"Yes." Miles presses his palms together, tapping his long fingers. "We've conferred and I'm the nominated spokesperson."

As Alice casts her gaze down to the multi-patterned carpet, I shrink a little behind Miles.

And he says it. "The cohort has spoken, and we don't think you and Piper are right for each other."

Danny does a double take. "Funny. I don't remember asking for your opinion."

Alice holds up her hands. "For the record, I'm not entirely agreeing. I really like Piper. I think she has good energy."

"It's not that any of us don't like Piper," I jump in. "It's more that we—"

"Can't stand her," Miles supplies.

"Miles," I snap. "We do like Piper, but you guys are always arguing, and I've seen her socials, Danny, it gets ruthless. About you." He folds his arms, and I forge on. "None of us like seeing you getting slammed on the internet and trolled by Piper's thousands of followers. Ultimately, if you're happy, we're happy. And we'd never want to get involved in your relationship, but maybe there's something you guys could do to improve the situation. Because the cycle keeps repeating."

He quirks an eyebrow. "It's not that bad. I just need to work on some stuff. Me stuff, you know?"

I frown back at him.

"I'm not a good person," he elaborates. "Piper's right about that."

The words stun me for a second, and I glance at Alice and Miles. "What do you mean?" I ask Danny.

He shrugs. "I'm just not a good person."

"Yes, you are," I tell him.

He doesn't respond.

We reach the front of the line, and Danny orders a Coke while Miles and Alice peruse the popcorn options. Waiting for his drink, Danny leans against the confectionary stand. I notice as he subtly slips a giant packet of M&M's into his jacket pocket.

I smack his hand, and he looks at me.

He shrugs and gives me a guiltless look, as if his eyes are saying, What? I told you so.

FAMILY GROUP CHAT

EVA: Hey! Do you miss me yet?

MOM: Yes! How are you?

DAD: House feels empty without you. How's the trip going? Have you been out on the water?

EVA: I miss you guys, too! Everything's going great. I have been out on the water, Colton let me borrow his board. You guys would love it here! I'll send some pics later.

DAD: Sounds great. We'll have to take a family trip sometime.

MOM: Be careful, hon. Stay with the group.

EVA: I will.

MOM: How's Miles?

EVA: Kind of quiet. Not himself. Do you think I should try to talk to him about everything?

MOM: That's up to you, Eva. Just be there for him. He's made a mistake and is paying the price.

EVA: Yeah. Cell service is bad out here. I'll call you when I can.

DAD: Have a good time, Ev.

MOM: Keep checking in! Remember those were the conditions, check in at least three times a day or we're driving down there.

EVA: Got it!

MOM: We love you. Be careful.

COLTON

It's getting late. The sky has darkened to bruise purple, and the low-watt porch light is barely hanging on. Noah's uncle left a couple of pots of paint for us, and Miles has been steadily working on the deck railings alone for the past hour, turning the posts from exposed wood to Harvest Moon White.

He musters a smile when he sees me approach.

"Hi," he says, then his eyes go back to the railings, and he drags his paintbrush carefully along the post, streaking the wood white.

"Hey. How's it going?"

He shrugs in response.

I don't know Miles all that well. He and Danny are tight, but I've never hung out with Miles one-on-one. I feel like I should say something more, get a conversation going, but I figure he's enjoying the quiet, so I follow his lead. Picking up a spare paintbrush, I get to work on the untouched railings.

The dusky bay stretches out before us with growing shadows bending over the water.

It isn't long before the others start to come out from the communal room. Noah and Piper are the first, Piper throttling a beer bottle and Noah carrying the crate. He packed the truck with a couple of boxes he *borrowed* from his dad's cellar.

One of the benches arranged on the deck creaks as Noah takes a seat and places the crate next to him. He pulls a bottle from the box and offers it to me.

I prop my paintbrush against the pot and take a seat.

"Do you want one?" Noah asks Miles.

Miles glances at Noah and the bottle in his hand, then shakes his head. "No, thanks. I don't drink."

"Fun," Piper mutters under her breath. She pulls an Adirondack chair closer, kicking her legs up on one of the railings that Miles hasn't reached yet. Her pale blue eyes wander over me, then she laughs, sharp and abrupt. "Lighten up, Colton. We're on vacation."

I frown. "What? I'm fine."

She smirks and rolls her eyes.

I don't know at what point Piper decided she didn't like me. Maybe it was around the time she started bad-mouthing my brother, and I called her out on it. It doesn't matter to me that she doesn't like me, but it always got to Danny back when they were dating. He couldn't wrap his head around it, how two of the most important people in his life didn't get along. He used to try to force us to hang out, and it never went well. Half the shit we spoke about ended up on social media the next day.

The patio door rattles open again, and Eva steps onto the

deck carrying a water bottle. She chooses the chair next to mine and burrows her hands into the sleeves of her sweater. "Hey," she says softly. "This is so pretty." Her eyes wander over the cove where oranges and golds bleed onto the horizon.

Our arms bump and I catch her gaze. She smiles, and I feel something. Something there between us that makes my heart beat differently.

"The deck is looking great, Miles," she says. His head stays bowed as he focuses on one of the paint-streaked posts.

"First coat should be dry soon," he says without looking up.

"I can help with the second coat tomorrow," Eva says.

The smell of paint merges with the salty air, catching in the back of my throat.

Piper snaps her fingers in Miles's direction. "Babe, why are you even still working out here? You've literally done more than enough, and it's getting dark. Come sit with us." She pats the seat beside her. "Loosen up."

I swear Miles grimaces as he puts down his brush and takes the Adirondack chair next to Piper.

She leans back in her seat and sighs. "You know, I actually think I've been converted to this place. Being at one with nature is so good for the soul, right?"

"That's what I'm saying." Noah clinks his bottle against hers. "So, you like it here now?"

"Obviously," she says with a sharp laugh. "I just said so, didn't I?" Then she raises an index finger, silver rings glinting in the porch light. "I still think it's lacking in amenities, though. I have my fake ID and cutest outfits, and no bars to go to." She exaggerates a pout. "Plus, I had a mission to find flings for all the girls."

Tension pulls at my neck. I know Piper's not going to be picking me as a good option for Eva. But I keep my expression the same, like it doesn't bother me.

Eva crinkles her nose. "A self-appointed mission," she says.

Piper gasps. "*Eva*. You should be so lucky to have me as your personal cupid. But, whatever. There's nothing here, anyway, so we'll just have to make the best out of our circumstances."

Noah's shoulders curl forward, and his face becomes lost in shadows. But I hear the smile in his voice, even if I can't see it on his face. "Sorry this private beach doesn't meet your standards, Piper."

She barks out another loud laugh. "That's okay, I'll forgive you." She starts tapping her fingernails on her Miller bottle. "Is it just me, or is anyone else at the point where they're just so ready to graduate?" Her eyes skim us—Noah, Miles, Eva, and me. "I'm done with high school and all the drama. I'm ready for college."

We all go quiet.

Miles's chin juts as he stares out at the dusky horizon.

"Yeah." Noah clears his throat. He pauses and takes a swig of beer, and his brow pinches like he's trying to think of something else to say.

Eva jumps in first. "So, Noah, does your uncle live in the area?"

"Yeah, he does," Noah says, relaxing. "He actually lives just outside of Portland, but he's always traveling. Paul's got some wild stories, for real."

"He's into extreme sports, right?" I add. Noah's uncle Paul met us at the property when we first came out here a few months back. He seemed like a laid-back guy with ripped jeans and grown-out sun-bleached hair. Nothing like Noah's parents, who are way more formal and uptight. They're all about academia and climbing the ladder in some corporation. It made sense to me then, why Noah looks up to his uncle so much. Deep down, he wants that life, too.

"Yeah," Noah answers. "He rafts, snowboards, cliff dives… You name it, man."

"Sounds like a cool guy," Miles says stiffly.

Piper takes a small sip of beer. "Totally." She dabs at her lips, blotting a smear of lipstick—that same bloodred color stains the rim of the bottle. "It's so sweet of him to let us use his place. Apart from the whole expecting free labor out of us mockery. No, thanks." She smirks. "But Miles has done an okay job out here, so if I ever meet the mysterious Paul, I'll just cheat and take the credit for his work."

She giggles, and we all fall quiet again. Eva glances at me, and I rub the nape of my neck.

In the silence, my eyes stray to the stone steps that lead down to the bay. "Eva." My voice sounds too loud. "Do you want to, uh, go see that beach drift I was telling you about?"

She frowns for a second. "What beach drift?"

"You know, the one I was telling you about."

A moment of understanding crosses her face. And a small smile. "Oh," she says. "Yes, the beach drift. Of course. Okay, sure."

We stand and I avoid the others' confused stares as we cross the deck and begin down the uneven stone steps.

A quiet laugh escapes her when we reach the sand. "Beach drift?" she whispers. "Nice cover."

I grin. "Yeah, I'm not good at thinking on my feet."

She stays close beside me as we head along the dune, footsteps sinking into the sand and our path lit by what's left of the dying sun.

"So, I'm guessing you wanted to talk in private?" she asks, her voice tentative.

"Yeah." I stuff my hands into my jacket pockets. "I wanted to tell you that I had fun with you today. I know it's been a while since we've hung out, just me and you, and…" My words fall away for a beat. "Yeah. I like hanging out with you."

"I had fun, too," she says softly. I glance at her, and she bites her lip as she smiles. My heart rate picks up.

We stop and sit on the dune, looking out over the rippling ink-blue tide.

"I was hoping maybe we could do more of this, if you want?" I glance at her again, and she nods. So I keep going, letting my messy thoughts spill out. "There's been times back home where I've wanted to talk to you…" I look at her again, watching for her reaction as I say the words. "In class, or at lunch, but it never feels right. And when Danny told me you were coming this weekend, it made me think… I don't know. There's some stuff I've been thinking about for a while."

"Oh?" she says, her eyebrows raising. "Like what?"

"Like I like you," I tell her, and my lips twitch. "I like being with you, talking to you, learning about you. I like who you are, always."

She breathes out a gentle laugh, and I can't hide the smile that's tugging at my mouth.

"That's so sweet, Colton," she says. Then after a pause, "I like you, too."

Now I'm grinning, bigger. "Yeah?"

"Yes," she murmurs.

She leans a little closer to me, and her hand brushes mine. I fold my fingers around hers, and she gazes down at our joined hands. When she looks up again, her golden eyes catch the slanted evening light.

I brush a strand of hair from her cheek.

"Oh, my god." The sound of Piper's voice makes us both jump. "Breaking news," Piper says, holding her camera toward us with the flash glaring. "Capturing this in real time, guys." She isn't talking to us; she's talking to her followers. "Colton Demarco and Eva Porta are literally about to hook up and I feel like such a voyeur right now."

Eva's hand slips quickly from mine, and she springs to her feet. "We were just talking." Her voice is flustered, embarrassed.

I drag my hands over my face. "Piper," I mutter. "Come on."

Piper's still holding her phone angled toward us. She starts bouncing on her toes. "This is so juicy! I'm obsessed! You guys are too cute."

"Would you stop?" Eva says through her teeth. "Please."

Piper lowers her phone. "Oh, shit. I killed the moment. Okay, listen, I'm just going to go back to the lodge and you guys can…" She waves her hand in circles. "Do whatever it is you were about to do. I'll warn everyone to avert their stares." She winks. "Be safe."

I grimace. "Piper, why—"

A panicked shout coming from the cabin cuts my sentence short.

FIVE MONTHS EARLIER

"You found the place, then?" A man with sun-bleached hair trapped beneath a backward ball cap is waiting to greet us outside the lodge. He must be somewhere in his forties, his eyes crinkling with a smile, and a sun-tanned face, even in winter.

I slip my keys into my pocket as we all get out of the truck, Danny, Javier, Noah, and me. Noah claps his uncle's outstretched hand and introduces us. Paul shakes our hands and pats our shoulders. We don't usually have Danny with us on a trip like this, but I figured it'd do him good to get out of Seattle. And away from Piper.

"So...?" Paul looks between us with a broad smile. "What d'you think of my latest investment?" He extends his arms toward the wild shoreline and log building before us.

"It's awesome," Noah says, smiling bigger than I've ever seen. And I get why. This place is something else.

"How could I resist, right?" Paul cuffs Noah's shoulder, then he leads us up to the deck and starts the tour. The wind is brutally cold, waves high and hitting the shore hard.

Paul directs us to the communal room and tosses us a couple of sodas from the fridge.

While Noah catches up with his uncle in the kitchen, Javier takes a seat next to me on the brown leather couch and slings his arms along the back. The log fire is already going, crackling away, and the wind is howling through the chimney.

I toss a cushion at Danny on the couch opposite, and he flinches.

"Get off your phone."

He grimaces, mouth turning down at the corners. "It's Piper," he says, flashing the screen at us over the coffee table.

Javier's thick eyebrows pull together. "Wait. I thought you guys were done?"

"We are," Danny mutters. "But she's texting me. She's pissed that I left town without telling her."

I launch another cushion at him. He ducks out of the way, and it hits the back of the couch. "She broke up with you," I point out.

"Yeah, but…" He returns his focus to his phone and starts typing out a message. Then he lifts his cell, waving it around, trying to get service.

Javier shakes his head. "Colton, we need to intervene. We need to help your brother." He aims a finger at Danny. "You've got to go ghost, man. Unless you want to get back together?"

"No, I don't. It wasn't working with us." But he's still typing.

The next thing I know, Javier's over the coffee table. He swipes Danny's phone and tosses it to me. "Confiscated," he says.

Danny heaves a sigh.

"Two days, no Piper," I tell him.

"Then when you're definitely over her," Javier adds, lifting his hand, "give her my number." He grins, flashing his teeth, and Danny musters a smile back.

Paul and Noah join us from the kitchen, and Paul tosses a couple more logs onto the fire. The flames hiss and spit embers onto the floorboards.

"So, guys weekend," Paul says, slapping his calloused hands together as he takes a seat next to Danny. "You don't mind me crashing?"

"Are you kidding?" Javier says. "You're letting us use your place." His eyes roam over the pine walls and antlers hanging over the fireplace. "Man, I want to live the life you got."

"You do, eh?" Paul cracks open a bottle of beer and points it at Javier. "Nothing stopping you, buddy. Key to success, work hard and go hard for what you want."

COLTON

I'm on my feet fast.

Just as I get to the deck, the door to the communal cabin swings opens and Karly runs out.

"You guys need to get in there, right now," she yells, gesturing toward the cabin.

"Oh, my god, why?" Piper calls, trotting up the stone steps behind me with Eva in tow. "What's going on?"

Karly flings her arm toward the communal room. "I think Javier and Danny are about to fight in there. For real."

And then I'm past her, throwing open the door into the cabin.

I cross the room toward them. "Whoa," I call. "What's going on?"

But neither of them looks at me.

Javier's hard stare stays on Danny. "I thought we were good," he says, sounding broken, defeated. "You said you were cool with Piper and me. I asked you, man, and you told me it was all good."

Danny's eyebrows pull together. "Yeah, and it is. I'm happy for you guys. It's whatever."

Javier lifts his hand, and I notice the piece of paper balled in his fist. "Yeah, it's whatever," he echoes. His grip tightens around the crumpled paper. "It's whatever."

Danny rubs the nape of his neck.

"But *I'm* the one who looks like a fool, right?" Javier keeps going. "Believing that this was over. It's never going to be over, is it?"

Everyone's in the room now, all eyes on Danny and Javier, watching, waiting for something more. An answer. Some explanation. Because earlier today everything was all good. There was no problem.

"What's going on?" I try again.

Javier glances at Piper, and she tucks a strand of hair behind her ear. Her face is drawn with the same confusion as the rest of us.

"What the hell, Javi?" she says, blinking at him.

But he doesn't respond. He just turns and walks away, leaving through the front door. With a sigh, Piper follows after him, shooting a questioning look at Danny as she passes.

When the door slams shut behind them, Danny's shoulders sink. He drops onto one of the couches and kicks his sneakers up on the coffee table. "Someone needs to rein that guy in," he says, pointing toward the door. "He's losing it."

I stay standing, staring at him. "What did you do?"

He swallows. "Nothing." But his eyes don't stay on mine.

GIRLS GROUP CHAT

KARLY: Piper, what's going on? We're in Eva's room. Come find us.

EVA: Is everything okay?

PIPER: Yeah. I'm in my room with Javi. He's heartbroken and confused about some note Danny left me.

ALICE: Oh, no. What note?

PIPER: I don't know, something Danny wrote and left in my room on top of my bag. Javier found it.

KARLY: What did it say?

PIPER: No clue. Javier threw it in the trash, and I can't exactly go get it while he's in the room with me! I'll come find you guys in a little while.

EVA: Okay, good luck. I hope you guys manage to figure everything out soon.

KARLY: Yeah, good luck. We love you.

EVA

Things have gotten a little awkward around the lodge. Miles and I are on one couch, and Karly and Noah are on the other. Danny and Colton have been in their room for the past couple of hours, and Alice ventured out to talk to Danny a little while ago. None of us have seen Piper or Javier since Javier retreated earlier, and the four of us remaining are pretending like we can't hear the muffled sound of them arguing through the thin dividing wall that separates us from their room.

Wind howls through the chimney and the antlers above the fireplace throw clawed shadows over the seating area.

"So…" Karly says, twirling a strand of ruby-toned hair around her index finger. "How about some music? It's kind of quiet in here."

Noah fumbles with his phone and sets the volume high. His playlist leaks out into the cabin, not quite loud enough to drown out the argument taking place in the adjoining room, or to make the awkwardness between *us* any less uncomfortable. In fact, the faint music on the edges almost makes our silence more painful.

There's a weird tension in the room—it's palpable. Probably because the topics we actually *want* to talk about, like college, our plans for after graduation, or whatever's going on with Piper, Javier, and Danny are politely off-limits. Plus, all the fighting has kind of killed the mood.

Alice steps into the cabin and closes the door behind her with a soft click. She crosses the room to join Miles and me on the couch.

I shuffle over to make space for her. "Hey. Did you talk to Danny?"

"Yeah. But I don't know." She fiddles with the end of her braid. "It's all a misunderstanding."

Miles and I swap a look. His sunburned brow furrows, a blush creeping below his hairline.

"What do you mean?" he presses.

"I'm not sure," she says, and her nose twitches. "Maybe you should talk to Danny."

"Are Colton and Danny just going to stay in their room?" Noah asks Alice, frowning. "They're not coming out here?"

She holds up her hands. "I don't know. Danny's keeping out of the way, that's what he said. But he hasn't done anything wrong," she adds quickly.

"Okay." Miles sighs as he stands. "This is weird. I'm going to go talk to him."

I hop to my feet, too. "I'll come with you." Of course, I want to talk to Danny and help straighten this mess out, but also I've kind of been waiting for an excuse to see Colton after how we left things on the beach.

As I follow Miles toward the door, Karly calls after us. "Let us know if you find anything out."

I give her a nod.

Miles and I move quickly along the outer corridor with the night wind streaming through the structure and the porch light weakly flickering.

We tread softly past Piper's room, shooting each other a look as we hear Piper's voice, "Well, maybe you got it wrong…"

And Javier's, "Got it wrong? Piper, come on…"

We hurry the rest of the way to Colton and Danny's room at the far end of the corridor, and Miles raps on the wooden door.

"Yeah?" Danny's voice comes back to us.

Miles leans in close to the door. "It's Miles and Eva."

A moment later, the door swings open and Danny steps aside to allow us in.

Their room is just like mine with two narrow beds flush against opposite walls, a woven rug covering worn floorboards, and a window looking out over the moonlit bay. In the darkness, the window reflects the room back at us with Miles and I lingering at the door, Colton seated on the edge of his bed, and Danny standing rigidly in the middle.

I notice a faint handprint on the glass, and something about the sight of it makes me shiver.

Danny takes a seat on his bed and the old frame creaks. "So, go on," he says, staring intently at Miles, then me, then

Colton. "Say whatever you've got to say." He rolls his hand, prompting us to speak.

Colton is silent, but his eyes stay on Danny.

"Okay," Miles says, drumming a finger on his chin with one arm folded across his slim chest. "So you wrote Piper a note? That's what people are saying."

"It's a misunderstanding." Danny echoes Alice's words—not that that gives us any clarity on tonight's events.

There's a beat of silence, and the wind whistles outside, tremoring the windowpane.

Danny rakes his hands through his tousled hair. "Look," he says calmly. "I know you all think I still like Piper. But I don't. Not in that way, and I think deep down, Javier knows that. It's his insecurity talking. We're just friends." He talks slowly, meeting each of our gazes as he says the words.

"Fine," I answer. "We believe you."

Danny looks at Colton where he's perched on the edge of his bed. Colton's sneaker is tapping quietly on the floorboards.

"But *you* don't believe me," Danny says, frowning at Colton. "What, am I not able to have friends of the opposite gender? Case and point." He gestures toward me. "Eva's my friend. So is Alice."

Colton presses his lips together and shrugs. "I'm not arguing with you," he says.

Danny grinds his teeth. "But you're looking at me like that." He flings his arm in Colton's direction.

"I'm not looking at you like anything."

"I haven't done anything wrong."

"But you've done *something*."

Danny groans into his hands and falls back onto his bed. His mud-spattered sneakers dangle over the end of the small frame.

Catching my gaze, Miles raises his eyebrows.

"Okay." I step in. "It's been a long day, we're all tired…" Danny groans again, and I forge on. "I suggest we put a pin in this, and you can iron out this *misunderstanding* with Javier tomorrow when everything's calmed down."

"I agree," says Colton, slapping his hands together.

Miles nods. "I do, too. Whatever you've done will blow over. Probably."

Danny stares up at the ceiling above his bed. He grabs the pillow from under his head and drops it over his face.

I glance at Miles again, and he shrugs.

"Okay, we're going to go," I say. "Maybe you'll come out and join us in a little while?"

"Maybe," Danny grunts, but the way he says it makes me think he has zero intention of leaving this room.

"See you," I call softly. "We're here if you need us."

"Yeah." Danny lifts his hand, but keeps his face beneath the pillow.

"See you," Miles echoes.

I offer Colton a small wave as Miles and I retreat out into the flickering porch light. Selfishly, I'd kind of hoped I'd be spending this evening with him—especially given how the night started. Too many years have passed since we last hung out, and I like learning about who he is now, the things that make him smile and laugh. I felt close to him today; it was natural and easy. Out on the water this afternoon, it felt special, and I'd been looking forward to continuing that tonight, especially after the moment we had on the beach earlier. Of course, that was before Piper interrupted, and Danny and Javier got into a fight and we were all thrown for a loop.

To my surprise, though, Colton follows us onto the deck. He closes the door behind him with a quiet click.

We pause in the corridor, all three of us.

Shadows cover Colton's face, darkening his eyes. "What do you think about all this?" he asks under his breath.

I look at Miles before I answer. "I believe Danny," I whisper back. "Regardless of what was written in this note, I believe him when he says he doesn't have feelings for Piper anymore." Colton runs a hand over his mouth, so I add, "I don't get that vibe from Piper, either. She's happy with Javier."

Miles raises his index finger. "But whatever Danny wrote to Piper was enough to hit a nerve with Javier."

"Yeah." Colton hesitates for a second, then adds, "He's been cheated on in the past. Maybe that's getting to him more than he's admitting. Trust issues, you know?"

We fall quiet for a moment.

"Something's up with Danny," Colton says at last, his voice lowered. "I know there's something going on with him. He's been acting off for the past couple of weeks, and I don't like the hold Piper has over him." He traps his lip between his teeth. "I don't think she cares about him, not like how he cares about her."

I sigh quietly into the night air. "Well, if that's true, then I'm sure Danny will figure it out eventually, the hard way. Let's just hope that whatever happened tonight will all blow over by tomorrow."

Miles stifles a laugh. "I admire your optimism, Eva. Alas, I suspect this is just the prelude to the main event."

★ ★ ★

Karly is already in my room when I get there. She's sitting cross-legged on Alice's bed and waving her phone in circles above her head.

I smile at the sight. "Trying to get cell service?"

"Always," she says. She checks the screen, then sighs before tossing her phone onto the bed. "So," she says, folding her hands in her lap and shuffling to get comfortable, "did Danny tell you what was in that note?"

I crawl onto my bed on the other side of the room and sit facing her. "No, but he says it wasn't how it seemed."

She combs her fingers through her hair. "He wouldn't say what he wrote, though?"

"No."

Her eyebrows knit. "Why not if it isn't a big deal?"

"Maybe he just doesn't want it to be misinterpreted again."

Her rosy lips purse. "Well, either someone's got this wrong or someone's lying."

I lean back against the wall. The mattress beneath me feels bumpy, and the comforter is itchy against my skin.

"Yeah," I murmur. "I guess we'll find out soon enough."

PIPER

ALBUM: SAVED VIDEOS

Hey, loves. Just checking in because, let me tell you, it has been a *night*. I won't bore you with the details, but I'll just say, I am beyond drained. I'm pretty sure everyone else is asleep, which is kind of disappointing. I expected more from our first night, but whatever. I guess I should go to bed, too, but I'm just taking a moment to soak up this beautiful place and be totally present. As you can obviously tell, it's dark out, so you guys can't actually see anything from this video, but it's so peaceful and grounding out here. I've really needed this.

Anyway, my trip is going so, so well and everyone's having the best time, which is perfect. I am a little concerned about one of my friends, though. And I just want to take a second to encourage everyone to find someone you can share your secrets with.

Someone you can trust. Guys, I know I say this all the time, but my DMs are always open, and I'm here for you.

It's actually funny because a lot of my friends think of me as their secret-keeper, I guess. Which is such an honor. Not everyone wants to share everything, though, and that's fine, too. It's okay to have secrets sometimes. I mean, unless those secrets hurt someone else, obviously. Those are the secrets that are going to need to come out, eventually.

But that's a whole different conversation. Maybe tomorrow.

Okay, I'd better go to bed now. Night, besties.

Love you!

COLTON

Darkness swallows the room, and the gale bats at the windowpanes, shaking the glass. Danny and Javier's fight ended the night early. But I haven't slept.

I reach over the edge of my bed and check my phone. The bright backlight makes me squint. The last text I sent is still highlighted on the screen. I'm sorry about what I said yesterday. I didn't mean it. The message has delivered, and Mom's replied.

I know. I'm sorry about everything, too. Have a good time on your trip.

I don't know why I always do it. Apologize. Like everything's my fault. Danny doesn't do that; he doesn't react in the way I do.

I lower my phone back onto the floor.

Danny's bed creaks. "Are you pissed at me or something?" His voice is tense in the darkness.

I breathe slowly. "No."

"Then why aren't you talking to me?" The bed creaks again.

"Because it's two in the morning and I'm trying to sleep."

"No, you're not," he mutters.

Our silence fills the room, broken by the distant sound of the tide and the wind howling through the forest.

"I texted Mom," I tell him.

There's a pause. "And?"

"I apologized to her."

He lets out a sharp breath. "Why, Colton? We're not the ones who should be apologizing."

I exhale into the darkness. Then, after a second, I ask him, "You're not lying to me about all this Piper stuff, are you?"

"No," he says. His voice wavers, though.

"You don't have to lie to me," I tell him, staring up at the shadowed ceiling. "You know that."

"Yeah."

"We agreed, right?"

He goes quiet, then. "I know," he says, and that's all he gives me.

EVA

Low sunlight streams through the bedroom window, striping the floorboards. Lounging on my bed and propped up with pillows, I turn a page in my book just as the door swings open.

I look up with a start and wedge my thumb between the open pages. Piper strides in, the heels of her leather boots clicking on the floorboards.

"Hey." Her eyes land on me, and she pauses. "Where is everyone?"

I close my book and set it down on the bed. "Some of them went down to the beach, and some drove into town to pick up supplies." I hesitate for a second. "Are you okay after everything that happened last night?" My question sounds a little forced. I can't help but feel some lingering frostiness toward Piper after she ambushed Colton and I on the beach last night. That was *our* moment, our first time talking like that. And I felt like I was floating along in a dream, until I realized it was being documented for Piper's live stream. This is all new territory for Colton and me, and I'm not even sure I know what it means, let alone for it to be subjected to public opinion. It makes me curl up inside to think that my parents might somehow get wind of me "hooking up" on a beach, after they put so much trust in me to come here unsupervised.

But Piper doesn't seem remotely aware of my clipped tone.

"Last night was such a disappointment," she says. "Like, on every level. This is supposed to be spring break, and it's so vanilla."

I squint in her direction.

"So everyone's just left?" she says. "Without me?"

"We thought you were sleeping. But Javier and the guys are only at the beach." I sit up straighter to peer out the window. Through the frame, I can see patches of blue sky and the glistening ocean. A little farther down the cove, there are some people at the shoreline, and some surfboards in the water.

"Still," Piper says, "they could have waited." She crosses the room and hops onto Karly's unmade bed, then she reaches across the nightstand for Karly's overflowing makeup bag. "Javier's obviously still upset," she says. The cosmetics clink as she roots through the bag. "It's like he thinks I'm going to end things with him or something. He's too in his head."

I soften a little at her deflated expression. "Sorry, that sucks."

"I know, right?" She pops open a compact mirror and begins quickly coating mascara over her dark lashes. "So, what's the situation with you and Colton?"

Heat rises to my cheeks. And now I'm mad at her all over again. "There is no situation. We're friends."

She glances at me over the top of the mirror and smirks.

"Stop. You can't pull that line on me, babe. I notice things, Eva. I'm an empath." She waves the mascara wand in my direction. "I feel it in the air."

"We're friends," I say again.

She points the wand at me. "Liar."

I feel hot suddenly. The thought of my private feelings toward Colton being broadcast over social media is giving me major anxiety.

"Okay, look," I change tack, "whatever your empath senses are telling you, can you just keep it between us, please?"

"Yeah, yeah. Totally." She returns her gaze to the compact and widens her eyes as she sweeps the mascara brush over her lashes. "Were you in his room last night?"

"No," I say quickly. "Well, technically, yes. For a minute. But only to talk to Danny about what happened between him and Javier."

Her eyes land on me again. "Yeah? What did Danny tell you?"

"Only that it was a misunderstanding, and that you guys are purely platonic."

"Oh. Okay." She returns her attention to her reflection. "Anyway, no offense, but I don't know what you see in Colton," she adds, dropping the mascara back into the makeup bag and popping the cap off a cherry red lip gloss. "Full disclosure, I can't stand him sometimes. You know he's the reason that Danny and I didn't talk for so long." She dabs on a layer of cherry gloss and smacks her lips. "He's got a problem with me, and he was always in Danny's ear stirring up shit between us. I actually think you're too good for him."

I stare back at her for a second. "I'm sure if Colton interfered with your relationship somehow, it wouldn't have been intentional. He's not the sort of person who'd deliberately make trouble."

She swivels around to face me and arches an eyebrow. "Eva, babe. Everything Colton does is intentional. The guy can't have a conversation without premeditating the whole thing. Don't you get that vibe from him?"

"No," I say honestly. "Not at all, actually."

"For real, I think Colton totally gaslights Danny, and that's why it never worked out between us." She glances at her reflection and combs her fingers through her shiny black hair. "Although, it all worked out for the best. Javier matches my energy way better. Also, he's a Pisces and I'm a Scorpio. Danny's a Sagittarius." She wrinkles her nose. "Not a good match." She aims the lip gloss at me. "What's your sign?"

"Leo," I answer.

"Oh."

I wait for her to say more, but she doesn't.

She rummages through the makeup bag again and tosses me a concealer stick.

I frown and place the concealer on the bed. "Piper, are you ever going to tell me what that text at the diner was about? Did it have something to do with Danny?"

She twists a strand of hair around her finger, then lets it fall into a loose curl around her face. "I don't know. Just some stuff people have been talking about, it's nothing." But the way she smiles into the mirror makes me think it *isn't* nothing.

She angles her face toward the light, inspecting the contours of her cheekbones. "But, yeah," she says, brushing a spec of mascara from beneath her eye. "Colton. You can do better."

EVA

Miles trudges behind me as I step over uneven stones toward a rocky outcropping hanging over the water, and the cave eroded into the face of the cliff. We head for the mouth of the cave, navigating a path through tide pools.

Low sunlight streams through the arched entrance, dancing on the pools. I hold my phone steady and take a couple of photos to upload to my family group.

I'm pretty sure my parents are the only people I know who get as excited as I do about tide-pooling.

"You're not actually expecting me to go into the cave, are you?" Miles gripes. "Because I have some health and safety concerns to flag, if so."

I crouch to the ground at the mouth of the hollow. "Ooh, purple shore crab," I report back to Miles, squinting in the low light as I glance up at him.

His arms stay tightly folded and his nose creases. "Mm," he says, with zero enthusiasm for my find. "Very nice."

"Come see."

"I'm fine, thanks."

I purse my lips as I gaze at him. "You're not having fun, are you?"

"*Fun* is a stretch," he says. Then he cracks a smile. "But this is better than hanging out with the others, I suppose. Marginally."

I frown back him. "I thought you liked everyone?"

"No, I do," he says, lowering himself onto the rock floor and sitting beside me. Water laps at the outcropping and he crosses his legs to avoid the spray. "But after last night, with all the theatrics between Danny and Javier, coupled with Piper constantly filming my every move…"

"Yeah, tell me about it." My focus strays out to the horizon and the slowly sinking sun. Colton, Javier, and Noah are out on their surfboards, evenly spaced along the bay. Everyone else is back at the lodge.

"The atmosphere has been weird today, hasn't it?"

Miles picks up a stone and scrapes it along the rock floor. "As expected. Danny and Javier have kept their distance, I've noticed."

My eyes stay on the surfboards. I watch as Javier springs into position and rides the curling wave. His hair is stuck down flat over his brow and the nape of his neck.

"Yeah," I murmur to Miles. "I was hoping they'd have talked it out by now. We're only here for one more night, and I'm not down for another replay of last night's awkwardness."

"I don't know," Miles says with a hint of a smile. "I quite

liked it." When I frown, he adds, "On a trip like this, I was anticipating drunk-and-disorderliness and all-nighters from these people, but we dodged those horrors last night."

I half laugh. "Well, that's true, I guess."

He presses his palms together and raises his hands skyward. "Thank you, Danny. Piper's been keeping her distance from Javier, too," he adds. Then he feigns another bright smile. "Hey, idea formulating. Do you think if I make Javier my new best friend and stick close, she'll keep out of my way, too?"

"You're really not vibing with Piper, huh?"

His chin juts. "She seems to get a kick out of reminding me about…" He lets the sentence taper off and his gaze lands on the frothing shoreline. "Everything," he finishes.

"I'm sorry," I say, trying to catch his gaze. Then as gently as possible, I add, "While we're on the subject, how are you?"

He tenses, avoiding my eyes. "I'm fine."

"Sorry," I say again, nudging his shoulder with mine. "I didn't mean to pull a *Piper* and remind you again. But since the conversation has presented itself, I just want you to know that I'm here if you want to talk."

He nods stiffly. "I know. And I don't."

"Okay. But if you do…"

He heaves a sigh as he turns to face me. "Eva, it wasn't me. Whatever you think you've heard, I didn't steal or sell any test papers. I didn't do it."

I hold my breath for a second, taken aback to hear him say these words out loud after nearly a full month of silence.

"I was expelled for something I didn't do," he grits out. "Someone set me up, and now I'm paying the price. And no one believes me."

"I believe you."

"Gee, thanks," he says, rolling his eyes.

I stare back at him, tilting my head.

"You sound like you're forcing yourself to believe me," he mutters. "Just like everyone else. Everyone loves the scandal."

"I don't," I tell him softly. "I never did."

His jaw clenches. "What does it matter, anyway? The school board already made their decision. I lost my place in Harvard, and I lost my future with it." He hops to his feet and brushes the grains of sand from his jeans. "We should go back now. I want to finish that second coat of paint on the deck before we lose the light."

"Miles," I murmur. But he's already started walking away, treading unsteadily over the rocks.

THREE WEEKS EARLIER

I sit higher in my seat, trying to peer across the library. Danny and I are seated at one of the tables lining the left wall, next to a tall window overlooking the football field and evergreens that surround the school campus. Open textbooks and notes are spread between us, taking up most of the workspace.

"Miles has been gone for a really long time," I say. "Lunch is nearly over."

Danny looks up from his paper. "We'll catch up with him later."

Our vice principal, Mr. Anderson, beckoned Miles out of the library about half an hour ago, leading him along the aisle of bookcases with quick strides and shiny shoes tapping on linoleum. Mr. Anderson had been fiddling with the end of his striped tie, a look of stress creasing his face.

When Miles left, Danny and I carried on working, and we've been quiet ever since, apart from the occasional buzz of incoming messages on Danny's phone. But as the minutes pass, I can't ignore the strange knot in my stomach whenever I think about Miles's abrupt departure. Or the stern expression on Mr. Anderson's face when he summoned Miles. Our typically laid-back vice principal didn't greet any of us in the same cheerful, jokey manner he usually would.

"What did Mr. Anderson need to see Miles about, anyway?" I wonder out loud.

Danny shrugs and taps his pen on his teeth. "Dunno. He probably needed him to run an errand or something."

That's a fair assumption. Miles always seems to have some sort of task or errand he's committed to. It's a weekly event.

Danny's phone buzzes in his hands. "Have you ever been to Tillamook State Forest in Oregon?" he asks.

"No," I say, slowly. "Why?"

"Noah Lauder's uncle bought a place near there," he says, his eyes still fixed on his phone screen. His thumbs are moving fast on the keypad even as he speaks. "I went with Colton and those guys a couple of months back." He looks up from his cell. "They're all going out there for spring break. Piper's going with Karly, and I think we should go, too."

My brow creases. "We, as in...us?"

He nods.

"Yeah, no," I answer. "I already have plans."

Danny stares at me and his lip curls. "You do not have plans, Eva."

I touch my hand to my chest. "Yes, I do. We do." I gesture between us. "Comic Con with Alice and Miles. You're supposed to be coming."

Danny's eyes are already back on his phone. "Comic Con isn't until the weekend. The trip is only two nights, Thursday to Saturday, so we'll get back to Seattle Saturday night and go to Comic Con on the Sunday. We'll only miss a day."

I mull over his words. "You might be able to convince Alice, but Miles won't like it."

"He'll be fine. He'll love it."

I glance along the aisle lined with bookcases. "I'm going to text him," I tell Danny. "I'm going to find out if he's coming back."

"Tell him we're going to Tillamook. And tell him to bring me back something from the vending machine."

"Okay." I unearth my phone from beneath my notes and type out a message to Miles.

Are you ever coming back?? Danny's trying to change our spring break plans. And he wants snacks.

"Done," I say, setting my phone down and returning my attention to my assignment. An AP algebra problem stares back at me with a disjointed muddle of sum reworkings marking the page.

My phone pings, and I reach for it.

The text displayed on the screen sends my heart into overdrive. "Oh, my god," I murmur.

Danny looks up and frowns. "What?"

My eyes move fast over the message. "Miles." Suddenly, I feel like I can't breathe. "I don't believe this. He's been kicked out."

Danny's eyebrows pull together. "What do you mean, he's been kicked out? Kicked out of what?"

"Of school." My pulse is racing, and I feel hot all of a sudden. "Miles has been accused of selling test papers. He's been expelled."

Danny falls back into his chair and his pen hits the table with a clatter.

GOOGLE SEARCH: Miles Brynne

A Seattle high school student has been accused of operating and profiting from selling stolen test papers. After allegedly selling the papers to senior students, seventeen-year-old Miles Brynne is awaiting consequences and could be facing prosecution.

Mrs. Lisa Garcia, the principal at the Seattle city high school, has given the following statement: "We are deeply saddened to find that a bright student full of potential has abused the education system in this inexcusable way. Rest assured that we have gone to great measures to rework and reschedule testing so that anyone who may have purchased these stolen papers will not affect the curve of the students who worked hard and honorably to study for their final exams."

EVA

The sun dips closer to the horizon, bleeding amber onto the cove. My conversation with Miles at the cave earlier has been weighing on me, but I'm not going to press it. At least, not tonight. We need one uncomplicated night, all of us.

My shoes sink into the soft sand, and I hug my water bottle as Colton and I head toward the group gathered at the bordering fir trees. We let the others go ahead while I found a signal-friendly zone to check in with my parents, and Colton waited.

He bumps his arm against mine as we walk. I get the feeling he's slowing his pace to keep on beat with me as we stroll along the beach.

"I wish we had more time here." His voice is lowered a little. I glance at him, and he smiles—kind of cute and lopsided. The slanted sunrays highlight the chestnut strands in his brown hair, and the deep shades of green in his eyes. A day of sunshine and salt water has brought out some freckles on his nose. I didn't notice them before, but I'm noticing now.

I catch some of my hair as the ocean breeze spirals it. "Me, too," I tell him. "I've had fun. With you," I add, feeling a flush rising.

He grins, and a dimple hollows his left cheek.

My gaze wanders over the bay with its rocky outcroppings and caves that fringe the silver ocean. The dying sun has gilded the shoreline, turning the white-capped waves rose gold.

I bring my eyes back to Colton and take a breath. "Actually," I begin tentatively, "I was thinking maybe we could find a way to have some time away from the others tonight." The blush creeps higher, so I carry on quickly, "It's just that it's our last night, and I want to be able to talk to you without it being documented on one of Piper's Instagram Stories."

He laughs under his breath. "I hear you. And yeah, if you want to leave the group tonight, I'll give it a few minutes and follow you. I'll meet you on the beach, by the cave."

A rush of excitement moves through me. "Okay."

"Okay," he echoes. Then he lowers his gaze to the sand, but he's smiling. His faded T-shirt ripples in the wind, and I can't help but notice the cut of muscles in his arms.

Okay, I think as butterflies flip my stomach.

The others have gathered on the sandbank, seated on salt-bleached driftwood at the edge of the forest. Noah crouches at the firepit, his ball cap pulled low and a matchstick balanced between his teeth. Beside him, Alice passes him more kindling. Her long black hair is fluttering in the salty breeze.

To the right of the firepit, Piper and Karly giggle, knotted together. Karly's scarlet-dyed plait has almost entwined with Piper's jet-black ponytail. Their laughter floats across the secluded cove, merging with the hiss of the tide and the whistle of the wind.

On the other side of the fire, Miles and Danny are sitting side by side on bone-white driftwood. Miles's shoulders are curled forward, shadowed by Danny's broader frame. Javier is sitting on the sand, kind of with the group but also kind of separate. His head is bowed, and his jersey hood is pulled up, covering his dark curls.

I tug on Colton's T-shirt before we reach the group, and he halts.

"Javier," I say under my breath, my gaze straying to the group on the sandbank. "How is he?"

Colton traps his lower lip between his teeth. "I don't know. I haven't had a chance to talk to him alone. But I will tonight."

"Piper says he's been down and distant with her all day," I murmur. "Maybe we can help them figure things out. Whatever was in that note, I honestly don't think Piper had any idea about it beforehand."

Colton's jaw clenches for a second. "Yeah. Let's just have a good night," he says. "Last night here." His easy smile returns, and he clinks his Miller bottle against my water.

"Last night," I echo, and something flutters inside my chest. I don't know if it's excitement, or apprehension, or both.

Whatever it is, it makes my heart skip a beat.

EVA

"Truth or dare, Eva?" Piper looks at me and smirks, her features morphing in the firelight.

I shift on my driftwood seat and fold my arms. "I already told you I'm not playing."

The contents of her Schnapps bottle sloshes inside the glass. "Girl," she says, and I hear the slur in her voice. "Not playing wasn't an option. The options were *truth* or *dare*." She aims the bottle at me and grins, teeth glinting in the moonlight.

I open my mouth to speak, to brush her off again because I know exactly how this will go. Truth: Are you and Colton a thing? Dare: skinny dip in the ocean. Neither of which I'm prepared to face.

But before I can speak, Danny jumps in. "I'll go," he says, and suddenly the voices around the fire quiet. The laughter stills, and the crackle of the flames sound louder all of a sudden.

Piper's lips crook into what I assume is a smile, but the

shadows twist it into more of a sneer. "'Kay," she says, direct-
ing the bottle at him now. "Truth or dare, Danny?"

"Truth," he answers. Everyone's eyes are on him, watching, waiting.

"Truth?" Piper quirks an eyebrow. "Are you sure about that?"
She barks out a laugh. "I mean, where do I begin, right?" She
drums her fingers on the bottle and her gaze skims the group.
Then she laughs again.

"Alright," Danny says, his nose twitching. "Dare, then.
Whatever."

A cold laugh escapes Javier, but he keeps his gaze trained
on the ground.

"Guys, come on," Noah says. "It's our last night."

"Thank god," Miles mutters under his breath.

Piper gives way to another giggle. Her eyes are back on
Danny and he rubs the nape of his neck.

Karly places a manicured hand on Piper's arm. She whispers
something to Piper, but Piper doesn't seem to react.

"So, what's it going to be, Danny?" Piper presses. "Truth
or dare?"

"Maybe we shouldn't do this right now," Alice says, wring-
ing out her hands. "Let's just hang out, chat. Like we've been
doing. We don't need to play games."

"Alice is right," I say. Colton's gaze lands on me through the
fire and I find myself echoing his words from earlier. "Let's
just have a good night."

There's a beat of silence, a charged tension between us, and
then Piper smiles.

"Boring," she sings. "But okay." She raises her phone and

snaps a picture in the darkness. The flash is like a firework in the night, stunning me for a second.

My eyes wander over everyone, noticing their expressions, their body language. Something is brewing—I can feel it. And I don't like it at all. The sooner I can leave the group, the better.

Ten more minutes. I'll give it ten more minutes and then I'm out. And hopefully, Colton will follow.

NOW
EVA

The piercing sound of a scream makes my breath hitch in my throat.

I'm alone, lost in the darkness. To my right, the flickering porch light marks the lodge, but the scream came from the moonlit cave in the opposite direction.

I stop still on the sand and listen.

Stones click. Footsteps move fast.

With my heart racing, I sweep my phone's flashlight across the bay.

"Hey!" I call out to them, whoever it is, or *was*, but my voice is swallowed by the night, and no one responds.

Slowly, I head for the cave, treading carefully over the slippery rocks while searching the bay with my tiny light, constantly scanning the shadows. Because someone screamed. Whoever it was, they might be hurt and needing help.

But I heard them run away, footsteps clicking over stones. At least, I think that's what I heard.

I step through the mouth of the cave.

"Is someone here?"

My question rebounds in the dank hollow. Clinging to my phone, I move my light in wide circles.

There's no one inside the cave, but there is a phone on the ground, probably left behind by whoever was last here—one of us, because we're the only ones around.

"Is anyone here?"

A shiver crawls down my spine.

So, I take the phone and I leave.

And then I notice the shattered screen.

"Hello?" I call again, but only the howl of the wind answers me.

EVA

I head for the flickering porch light.

Back in the path of light, I feel calmer. Safer. It's too easy to get weirded out in the dark. It had to have been one of the guys messing around in the cave, trying to scare us again. If I take the cell back to the lodge, I can leave it out for someone to claim. They won't miss it tonight since the signal around here is so patchy, anyway. And it's got to belong to one of them. It's not as though we've seen anyone else in the area. This is privately owned land, and it isn't exactly easy to get to from the road. It took us a couple of wrong turns on narrow dirt tracks until we finally found the right lane.

My shoes sink into the sand as I near the little log-walled cabin on stilts. I climb the stone steps leading to the wrap-around porch overlooking the dark beach. Fireflies whizz around my head, shooting dangerously close to the electric bug zapper crackling above the patio door.

The shadowed silhouette of someone seated on one of the deck chairs makes me stop. He knots his hands and leans forward, and the night breeze stirs his hair. "Hey," he says.

I squint in the weak porch light. "Danny?"

"Where've you been? You left the fire ages ago." He launches a pebble and I hear it thud softly on the sand below.

"Yeah. I overshot." I pause for a second, glancing toward the moonlit shoreline. "Were you at the cave just now?"

He frowns. "No. Why?"

"I just thought I heard someone around there. I thought I heard a scream, actually."

"Wasn't me," he says. "I've been back for a while. And I didn't hear anything from here."

The bulb flickers, blinking us in and out of darkness.

"Okay," I answer. "Maybe I'm imagining things. But I did find a phone in the cave. I assume it isn't yours?"

He lifts his cell in response, and I recognize the blue magnetic case.

"Never mind. It must have been one of the others. Are they still at the fire?" *Is Colton?* I want to ask.

"Some of them. But—"

He stops short. The sound of laughter and voices reaches us from the beach below the veranda, and Alice and Miles trot up the stone steps.

"Hey!" Alice skips onto the porch, her shoes tapping over the planks. She wraps her arms around my shoulders. Her hands are lost inside the sleeves of her oversized sweatshirt. "Where've you been? Miles and I have been looking for you."

"Apparently, my sense of direction is a little off," I say wryly. "By the way, I found someone's cell in the cave—it didn't look like either of yours, though…did either of you lose your phone tonight?"

Miles pats his jeans pockets. "Not mine."

"Mine, either," Alice says. Her arms slip from me, and she gives a little shiver. "Can we go inside? It's freezing out here."

"Yes, please." I glance back at the moonlit beach. There's no sign of Colton. If he does show up, I guess he'll come find me. "But I think I'm going to go to bed," I tell Alice as I thread my arm through hers. She nods, and we head for the door. Miles trails dutifully behind us. Only Danny doesn't move.

"Night," he calls as the three of us bustle into the main cabin.

As Alice flips the light switch in the communal room and Miles starts rooting through the fridge, I cross the rustic living area, calling good-night as I head out through the front to access the rooms leading off the external corridor.

Pacing quickly along the deck, I slip into my room and close the door. Karly's bed's empty, but the window is open and a breeze is billowing the floral curtains. When I reach out to pull the window shut, I glimpse the faint image of a face mirrored off the glass.

My breath catches.

It's *my* face. It takes a second, but a small laugh escapes me. I must be seriously tired if I'm spooked by my own reflection. Still, I quickly drag the latch across, bolting the window with a thump. Then I plant myself on the bed and prepare to wait for Colton.

The sound of voices drags me from sleep.

I roll over in the firm bed and push the loose strands of

hair from my face, squinting in the new light. It takes me a moment to remember where I am.

Sunbeams are streaming through a gap in the curtains, coloring the wood-clad room. And a faint blue tint pulses on the floorboards and woven rug.

I sit bolt upright. Karly is sleeping soundlessly in the single bed across the room. Her Burberry suitcase is propped against the pine frame, spilling over with clothes. The stone-gray shirt she was wearing last night is slung over the back of the wicker chair.

I untangle myself from the itchy comforter and stumble to the front window. Outside, police are cordoning off the gravel path leading to the lodge. And EMTs are loading a stretcher into a waiting ambulance.

"Karly." My voice sounds raspy. "Karly, wake up."

She makes a noise and rolls over.

My heart starts galloping in my chest. "There are police outside." I trip over my words. "Something's happened."

Suddenly, she's alert. Her bed creaks as she jumps up and hurries to the window, her oversized T-shirt still twisted at the waist.

"Oh, my god," she whispers. She grips my hand. Her nails dig into my skin, but I barely feel it.

On the stretcher, a white sheet is drawn over the contours of a human face.

COLTON

She's standing on the shoreline, the woman. The cop.

I almost didn't notice her on the beach, waiting on the strip of sand below the lodge. She waves me into shore.

I lay flat against my board and paddle, dragging my arms against the current. She's probably going to write me up for surfing in a prohibited area or some shit like that. This seems like the kind of beach that'd be off-limits. The rocks around the bay might as well be barbed wire.

I woke up early, restless. I messed up last night. I saw Eva leave the fire, but I couldn't bail on Javier right when he'd started to talk, and by the time I got back to the lodge, Alice told me Eva had already gone to bed.

At the shallows, I stand and wade the rest of the way back to shore. My feet sink into the wet sand.

"Hi there. Detective Brennan." The cop introduces herself with a flash of her police badge. Then she hesitates, just for a beat, her stare roaming over my face as though she's trying to figure out where she knows me from. "Can I take your name, please?" She's holding a silver pen and a notepad. Her eyes dart between me and the lined paper. She's a couple of inches shorter than me, somewhere in her thirties, blond ponytail bobbing in the wind. She's petite, but she's got this hard look in her eyes. This don't-test-me look.

"Colton Demarco," I answer. My voice is scratchy from salt water. My hair's stuck to my eyebrow, water dripping from my temple and crawling down to my jaw.

I face her, board jammed into the wet sand and the frothy waves breaking over my ankles. "I'm sorry, I didn't know this area was restricted."

"Are you aware that there's been an incident here?" she says. "Last night."

"What?" My stomach lurches. "What incident?" Thoughts start coming in fast. Danny wasn't in our room when I left this morning, he wasn't in his bed. And Eva. Alice said she was in her room, but the door was closed...

The cop is talking, and I'm trying to take it in. Trying to focus.

"Are you local, Colton?"

I push the wet hair back. "No, I'm from Seattle. I'm staying at my friend's uncle's place. Right over there." I point to the raised log cabin, and the rocky steps leading up to it from the beach.

She follows my gaze. "Why don't you go on back to your accommodation please, Colton." She uses my name like she knows me. Like she's on my side. But I hear the opposite.

"Yeah," I say. "Sure. What's going on?"

"I can't really give you any details right now, but I'll be coming to the property shortly to get some more information. In the meantime, I'm going to need you to sit tight."

"We're supposed to leave today."

She doesn't respond.

My shoulders tighten. But I nod, mostly to myself, and I follow her across the beach toward the lodge. My board digs into my ribs, wearing on my skin with every step I take in the sand.

When we near the place, she heads for the gravel path at the front. I see people gathered on the track. An ambulance, cop cars, orange cones.

My chest heaves.

This isn't good.

COLTON

The cop, Brennan, walks over to the cones and starts talking to two guys in uniform. One's tall with sharp features and pale skin. The other guy is older, with gray stubble and thin white hair that moves in the breeze. The wind is picking up, ice-cold and stinging my wet skin.

I jog up the wooden porch steps and prop my board against the outer wall. Breathing hard, I throw open the door to my room. It's empty. Danny's bed is exactly as it was before we left for the fire last night.

My head's spinning, thoughts coming in wild. The way Brennan looked at me when I came to shore, it was like she'd seen my face already. The way she faltered, like she was seeing a ghost.

I stumble from the room and start banging on doors.

Eva's the first to come out, and relief shoots through me. I see her in the corridor, shrugging into a sweatshirt. Karly is right behind her, her hand pressed to her mouth.

"Hey," I call to them. "Are you okay? Something's happened."

Eva looks beyond me to where the police car is parked in the clearing and Brennan is in conversation with the other cops. "What's going on?" she whispers, her eyes searching mine.

I shake my head. "I don't know."

Karly folds her arms tightly around herself.

Eva lowers her voice. "We saw someone…" The words tremor and she takes a breath. "Someone was taken away on a stretcher. There was an ambulance. Did you see?" Her eyes dart back to the cordoned off road, and the cops.

"No." My pulse is thundering in my ears. "Have you seen Danny? He wasn't in our room this morning."

Eva's face falls.

More doors start opening, and the others begin to step out, blinking, squinting, barely awake. Miles, Alice, Javier, Noah…

I'm asking the same questions. *Have you seen Danny? Did he come back last night?*

Then Karly starts asking questions, too. I hear her voice above my own. "Where's Piper? Oh, my god," she says breathlessly. "Where's Piper?"

My eyes shoot to Javier, and he stills.

"Where's Piper?" Karly asks again.

The sound of boots crunching over earth makes us stop.

Detective Brennan climbs the wooden steps to join us on the deck. The two other cops are pulling yellow tape between the cones, blocking access to the road.

Eva moves closer to me, and her fingers thread through mine. We all just stand there, staring.

Brennan flashes her police badge. It glints in the low sunlight. "Good morning," she says. She isn't smiling. "We're following up on an incident that was reported early this morning, and I'm going to need your cooperation while we investigate the circumstances."

I'm trying to listen, but my head is spinning. My eyes are constantly moving, searching the cove for him. I want to check our room again, just in case, but Brennan is watching me. Holding us here.

She looks slowly between us. "Is this everyone?" she asks.

Eva's grip tightens around my hand.

"No." My voice sounds hoarse. "My brother is missing."

"And our friend Piper," Karly adds, unsteadily. "We don't know where they are."

Brennan nods. "Okay. I'd like to talk to you each individually, one at a time," she says, and her stare travels to the communal cabin at the other end of the corridor. "Perhaps inside."

When no one speaks, her focus lands on Eva. "Would you like to go first?" Brennan asks with a thin smile.

"Yes," Eva murmurs. "Yes, okay."

Brennan gestures for Eva to lead the way, and her hand slips from mine. Helpless, I watch her walk away.

The next thing I know, the older cop is signaling to us from the clearing, gesturing for the rest of us to come down. And all I can do is follow, numb.

Title: Audio File_Eva Porta Interview

Recording commenced at seven forty-five a.m. on Saturday, April sixteenth. Can I take your name, please?

Yes. It's Eva. Eva Porta.

Hi, Eva. My name is Detective Brennan, and I'm going to be asking you a few questions about last night. Does that sound okay?

Yes. Yes, of course.

Why don't you talk me through your actions between the hours of seven p.m. last night and seven a.m. this morning.

Sure. Um, last night we had a campfire on the edge of the forest.

I'm going to need some names here, Eva.

Oh. Yeah. Myself, Colton, Danny, Miles, Alice, Karly, Piper, Javier, and Noah. Everyone staying at the house. It's Noah's uncle's property. His name's Paul, I think. Paul Lauder.

Okay. Eva, how was the mood amongst your friends last night?

Fine, I guess.

You guess? That's quite a vague response. Why don't you try again.

No, it was good. Everyone was fine. It's just that our friends… Javier and Piper, they're a couple, and they'd been arguing. But it wasn't an issue.

What were they arguing about?

I don't know all the details.

But you know some details, I presume?

It really wasn't a big deal. Javier found a note that someone wrote to Piper, and I think it made him feel a little insecure. I'm not sure, I don't know.

I see. And did their fight escalate through the night?

No. It wasn't a fight, not really. Um, I should mention… I left the group ahead of the others, and I heard a scream when I was walking back. I looked around but I couldn't find anyone. It came from the cave, I think.

At what time was this?

Around midnight.

And you were alone when you heard this scream? Is there anyone who can vouch for your whereabouts?

I… No. But I saw my friend Danny just a few minutes later. He was out on the deck when I got back.

Was he alone?

Yes. I mean, I think so.

You said you left the group before anyone else. Why was that?

I… I don't know. I guess I was just tired.

How is it that your friend Danny was at the property ahead of you, if you left before him?

I don't know. I waited on the beach for a while, alone.

I see.

And when I heard the scream, I went to look. I went to the cave. I heard someone running over the stones, too. That's what it sounded like, anyway.

So, you say you heard a scream and running, but saw no one? That seems strange, doesn't it?

Uh... Yes. But it was dark. I only had my phone light. My battery was dying and...

Right. No one else heard or witnessed this scream?

I don't know. I don't... There was no one else around.

Okay. Anything else? Any other details you may not have mentioned? (0:14 DELAY) Eva?

No. Nothing that I can think of right now.

EVA

I just lied to the police.

My heart's beating fast as Detective Brennan switches off her recorder and clips it to the holster on her belt. Her light hair is scraped into a ponytail and her gold PD badge is hanging around her neck. She offers me a tight smile.

I fold my hands in my lap and try to control my breathing. We've been alone in the communal room while she recorded my statement, sitting opposite each other on the tan leather couches around the fireplace.

Everyone else is outside with another police officer.

Everyone except Piper and Danny.

Detective Brennan stares at me from across the coffee table. It's still cluttered with plates and plastic cups from last night. Beer bottles, too. "If there's anything else you think of," she says, tilting her head, like she's waiting for me to break.

I cross my legs and the phone in my pocket presses against

my hip. Not my phone; the mystery phone that I found in the cave and forgot to leave out for its owner. The phone that, if I'm caught with it, will undoubtedly make me look even more suspicious than I *clearly* already do.

Is there anyone who can vouch for your whereabouts? Detective Brennan's words echo loudly in my mind. *You say you heard a scream and running, but saw no one? That seems strange, doesn't it?*

I swallow hard.

"If there's nothing more," she adds, "then I think we can finish up here for the time being."

Morning light streams through the windows, making me squint. "Two of our friends are missing," I manage. "Their names are Danny Demarco and Piper Meyers. They were both here last night, but neither of them were in their rooms this morning."

She nods slowly, her eyes never leaving mine. "I understand." There's no shock or urgency in her response.

My lungs feel like they're constricting, shrinking. "Do you know where they are?"

"Unfortunately, I can't answer any questions right now," she says, her expression unreadable. "But thank you for your help, Eva." She stands, waiting for me to do the same.

I rise to my feet. "Okay," I murmur, and she gestures toward the front door, expecting me to leave. But I don't. "Can you tell me why we're being questioned?" My voice sounds weak. I feel it. "Is someone…" I can't bring myself to say the word. The memory of the body on the stretcher makes my breath quicken. The white sheet drawn over the face. The thud of the ambulance doors closing.

We stand on either side of the huge fireplace, facing each

other. A shadow of something close to sympathy crosses her face. "I'll be able to answer your questions soon, once I have confirmation and authorization to do so. In the meantime, I'm going to need you to sit tight."

A wave of nausea comes over me and I glance at the clearing beyond the front window. The others have gathered at the bordering fir trees.

My eyes land on Alice, but I know she can't see me from out there. I wish she could. I wish we were back in my room in Seattle, giggling over our failed TikTok attempts, or binge-watching Netflix shows. I wish I could tell her that I'm sorry for convincing her to come on this trip. Miles, too. I shouldn't have gone along with Danny. None of us were supposed to be here.

We should be at Comic Con right now, probably grabbing breakfast from a food stall. Alice would be sketching passersby in their cosplay outfits, and Miles and Danny would be arguing about fantasy world terminology. We'd be laughing. We'd be together.

In this reality, Alice and Karly are huddled close with their hands joined. I know Alice will try to stay strong for everyone, supporting Karly while we wait for Piper to show up. But beneath the front, Alice will be scared, too, just like I am. Scared for Piper. Scared for Danny. Scared, period.

My focus wanders to Javier and Noah. They're talking between one another, their heads dipped. Javier's palms are pressed to his brow, and Noah's ball cap is pulled low, shading his face, and trapping sandy blond curls around his ears. Opposite them, Colton and Miles are standing side by side, Colton's dark hair still damp with seawater. For a split second, I almost see Danny.

I'm so used to seeing Danny and Miles, or Danny and Colton, that my brain can't compute seeing both of *them* without *him*.

In the spot in the clearing where the ambulance had been, an unmarked car is parked, obstructing the track that leads through the forest, blocking the exit for the Demarcos' truck and Karly's Prius.

My gaze snags on the Prius for a moment. I can almost hear the echoes of our laughter from two days earlier. The feel of the front passenger seat as we cruised along the forested highway, passing a bag of Skittles back and forth between the four of us. Karly behind the wheel, her fire-red hair fluttering in the breeze from the open window. The smoky scent of Piper's perfume whenever she leaned into the front to turn up the volume on the stereo or change the station. And Alice, smiling uncomfortably whenever Piper directed her phone's camera her way.

"Does that sound okay, Eva?" Detective Brennan's voice jolts me, and I bring my focus back to her.

I take a small breath. "Yes."

"For now, I suggest you—" Detective Brennan cuts her sentence short when her radio crackles. She raises her finger, signaling for me to wait. Then she lifts the radio to her mouth and murmurs into the speaker. She steps away, heading for the front door. Her shiny shoes click on the floorboards.

The faint sound of a car engine comes from outside.

"Just wait right here one moment, please," Detective Brennan calls to me. She leaves the cabin just as another police car pulls up along the road.

I hurry to the window and grip the ledge. All I can do is stare, waiting, watching as the engine cuts and an officer gets out of the driver's side. He walks around the car and opens the back door.

I hold my breath, my eyes fixed on the car as I try to catch a glimpse of the person in the back.

TWO WEEKS EARLIER

The final bell has already gone, and the upper hallway is eerily deserted. My footsteps tap a quick rhythm as I leave through the main exit out onto the quad. My car is just ahead, one of the few remaining, but as I near the parking lot, I notice two familiar figures standing outside the sports storage room around the side of the school.

Danny and Piper. Their heads are bowed in conversation.

They're not in my path, but I deviate and head toward them. I step up behind them and realize a moment too late that I've walked into a private moment.

"...this is so bad," Piper says, chewing her manicured thumbnail.

Danny's voice sounds choked. "I know. We never should have—"

Piper notices me and immediately nudges him. He stops short. His face drops when he sees me standing behind him. I frown, and his Adam's apple bobs. He looks sick all of a sudden.

"Hey," I say slowly. "Sorry, did I interrupt something?"

Piper blinks in surprise. I don't think I've ever seen her this lost for words. "Eva," she says, forcing a smile. "Hi."

"Hi."

There's a long pause.

"Is everything okay?" I ask, looking between them.

They swap a glance, and I swear Danny's eyes turn almost pleading.

"Yeah," Piper says at last. "Everything's fine. We were just talking." She runs her fingers over her silky hair.

My eyebrows knit. "Okay. I guess I'll leave you to…" I wave my hand in their direction. "Talk, or whatever."

Neither of them speaks, and I walk away. Not my business.

COLTON

A squad car pulls up along the dirt track on the other side of the clearing. At the same time, Detective Brennan comes out of the cabin. She's holding her radio to her mouth, talking into it as she walks quickly over the planked deck and down the wooden steps. Ocean air ripples her uniform.

Eva isn't with her. I can see her, though. She's still inside the cabin, standing at the window. But she isn't looking at me. She's looking at the cop car.

I breathe slowly.

"It's him," Miles says, gripping my arm.

I barely hear him over the sound of my heart thumping in my ears. Numb, I watch Danny climb out of the car, and the air releases from my lungs. He looks right back at me, like he's trying to tell me something. Like he thinks I already know.

None of us move for a couple of seconds. Karly and Alice, Noah and Javier, Miles and me. We all stand tensely, just staring at Danny, and at the car, wondering if Piper is going to get out next. But the cop closes the back door and Danny starts making his way toward us.

Brennan stays at the car with the driver, deep in discussion. But my eyes don't leave Danny.

When he reaches us, his jaw clenches.

"Hey," he murmurs. His voice is too quiet, and his eyes are red.

I can't speak. I just keep breathing.

"Hi," Miles says quickly. "Are you okay? What the heck's going on?"

Danny looks at Miles, then at me. No one else. Alice, Karly, Noah, Javier, they're all trying to catch his gaze. But he won't look at them.

"Where's Piper?" Javier's voice sounds rough. The muscles in his jaw are tight.

Danny casts his eyes downward.

Alice's hand stays knotted with Karly's. "We woke up this morning and there were police everywhere," she says. "And you and Piper were gone. We didn't know what had happened."

"They haven't told us anything," Karly whispers. The gale whips at her hair, and she looks fragile enough that it could knock her over. "We don't know where Piper is. We don't know what's going on."

Another murmur of wind moves through the trees, whistling as it bows the branches.

Just say it, I think. Because I know it. I feel it. We all do.

Danny starts breathing fast. He's trying to speak.

I grip his shoulder. Because he needs me to. I need it, too.

"I found her this morning," he says. "She's dead."

PIPER

Hi, loves. So, I know I said I wasn't going to do a Live today, but I just feel like I need to off-load—know what I mean? It's really important to have that safe space to talk, you know? I feel like I'm having a pretty bad day, school was so *meh* today, and to be honest, I'm on a bit of a downer because I've lost a lot of trust in people lately. It's super hard. Sometimes, when that line is crossed, when you see another side to someone, it's impossible to unlearn that, right? It changes everything.

I can see some of you guys commenting here, asking if I'm okay, and that's so sweet of you. I am okay, I'm just having a day. But, on a more positive note, because you know I'm positive-vibes only, I'm so excited for my spring break trip next week, and maybe I'll explain this rant a little better once I've had time to process.

Actually, that's a really good idea. Comment if you think I should do, like, a PSA video kind of thing. Maybe I could stitch with some of my friends, and we could do a whole truth-circle vibe.

Okay, I'm inspired—yay! Love you, besties!

COLTON

"Piper didn't come back to the rooms last night." Danny keeps his voice low, hands shoved in his pockets. "After the fire," he mutters. "She never came back."

The rest of us are silent, just listening to him. I'm trying to breathe. Slow. Controlled. But I'm looking at him, wondering.

"You all did." He looks around, his eyes landing on each of us. "You all came back. I waited up," he says, swallowing. "When it started to get light, I went out to look for her. And I…" He halts his sentence and rubs his eyes with the heels of his hands. "She was in the cave. At the back, there's a steep drop into a ditch, and she must have fallen. The tide had flooded it. She was facedown, not moving."

My pulse is slamming in my ears while I listen to his story. Karly's hand is pressed to her mouth, and she and Alice are tangled together, their hands locked. Noah is gripping Javier's shoulder. And Javier…he looks like he's about to drop to the ground.

"So, I got her out. Then I went out to the road," Danny murmurs. "I called an ambulance. But it was too late."

Alice presses her fingers to her lips. "Oh, my god," she whispers, her eyes pooling. "Danny, I'm so sorry."

Javier takes a sharp breath through his teeth. He links his hands behind his head, knotting his fingers through his curls. "No." He manages to speak. "No, this can't be happening."

Noah keeps his grip on Javier's shoulder, like he's holding him upright.

The crackle of a radio interrupts us as Brennan approaches. I run my hand over my mouth.

"Thank you for waiting," she says flatly. Her eyes move over Danny, and Danny looks down at the ground. His sneakers are wet, along with the bottoms of his jeans. "As I'm sure you're now aware," Brennan says, "I can confirm that a teenager named Piper Meyers was found unresponsive this morning. Despite the efforts of our paramedics, Piper did not regain consciousness and was pronounced dead at the scene."

No one speaks, just quick breaths and sharp inhales. Karly sobs quietly into her sleeve.

"Given the severity of the incident," Brennan says, "I can't permit you to leave the state at this point. I'd still like to talk to each of you. Hopefully, with your input, we can make sense of how this tragic accident occurred." Her eyes are on me now, and she gestures toward the lodge, where Eva's shadow still waits at the window.

I keep breathing slowly.

Brennan offers the others a cursory glance. "I appreciate

this is a distressing time for you all, and I'd like to thank you for your cooperation in the investigation. We have a phone number for a trauma group on hand to help you through this difficult time."

The words are all there, but I don't hear sympathy. I hear something else. And I see it in the way her eyes travel over us, narrowing as she assesses our reactions, trying to figure us out.

She said it was an *accident*—that was the word she used. But the way she's talking to us, looking at us, her words and her actions aren't adding up. This place is so isolated; there's no one around. If this wasn't an accident—if they think somebody did this—then she knows it was one of us.

Title: Audio File_Colton Demarco Interview

My name is Detective Brennan, and the time is approximately eight forty-five a.m. on Saturday, April sixteenth. For the purpose of the recording, please state your full name.

Colton Demarco.

Thank you. Colton, I'd like to ask you a couple of questions about your friend Piper Meyers. Does that sound okay?

Yeah.

Your brother, Danny, was the person who found Piper unresponsive this morning. I understand he had a romantic relationship with her, too. Is that right?

Yeah, he did. But that was a while ago. Months ago. She moved on since then.

Piper moved on? But Danny didn't?

No, I didn't mean that. Danny moved on, too. We're all on this trip together, and Piper is with Javier now. It was all good.

Okay. Talk me through what happened here last night.

We had a fire on the beach, we just hung out for a while. Then we came back to the lodge and went to our rooms. I woke up early to surf, and now I'm here.

Let's go back to last night. Where were you at around midnight, Colton?

I was with my brother; we came back to the room at about that time.

That's interesting. It was my understanding that your brother, Danny, was seen back at the property at midnight, and he was alone.

He wasn't alone. He was with me.

It seems strange that your friend saw him alone, though, doesn't it?

I was with him. It was dark, and the outside lights don't work all that well. You can test them, if you want. They're always cutting out.

I'll take your word for it. What about your friend Javier, and the disagreement he had with his girlfriend, Piper? Can you weigh in here?

I don't know anything about that. Sorry.

COLTON

The cop keeps tapping her fingertips together while I talk. I don't know if she's trying to throw me off, or distract me from my story, but I see it.

The leather couch squeaks as she moves. She folds her slender hands together.

She hasn't said the word *murder* yet.

I try to read her steady expression, to figure out what she's thinking when she's looking at me, when she's listening to me talk. They've probably pulled our records already. They probably have all our names and histories. They won't find much on me, or Danny. But they'll know that we were on the CPS register.

My mom went through some stuff a while back. Single mom, fired from her job, couple of bad relationships, and a few missed appointments. Social workers used to come to the house, ask us questions, and we learned fast that we had to play a role. We had to give nothing away, but act like we had nothing to hide. It's a skill I got really good at. Danny did, too.

That's why the tapping doesn't throw me off. The sympathetic head tilt doesn't, either. I just keep talking like I've got nothing to hide.

On the inside, though, my heart feels like it's about to bust through my rib cage. Brennan switches off the recorder and clips it to her belt.

"Thank you, Colton," she says. Her paper-thin smile doesn't reach her eyes.

She stands, and I take the cue.

My eyes stray across the room. There are empty beer bottles on the kitchen counter. All of us are underage, but that's the least of our problems right now.

She follows my gaze to the bottles, then her eyes come back to me. "Were you and your friends drinking a lot of alcohol last night?"

I've been asking myself the same question.

"Spring break, isn't it?" she says, her sharp eyebrows lifting, telling me *I'm just like you*. "Believe it or not," she adds, "I was a senior in high school, once."

I furrow my brow, playing the game. "I don't think anyone drank too much. None of us are like that."

Her pale lips press into a smile. Or a grimace.

I had this feeling before we left for the trip, this gut instinct that nagged at me while I was strapping the surfboards into the truck's cargo bed. I'd stopped for a minute, letting the sun beat down on my neck.

I'd almost backed out. But I'd fought with my mom the

day before, I'd said some things, and I needed to get away, to escape my life for a while.

I shouldn't have run, though. I shouldn't have let Danny run, either. Because now we're here, and it's worse.

Brennan leads me back outside onto the deck. Noah's uncle Paul is here now. He's across the clearing talking to the police and gesturing toward the coastline, one hand knotted through his shaggy, sun-bleached hair. The others are all right where I left them, but Eva is with them now, too. She's with Miles and Danny on one side, and Noah, Javier, Alice, and Karly are on the other. It's as though there's some invisible divide between them, holding them apart. Tears are streaming down Karly's face, and strands of red hair are clinging to her pale cheeks. Alice's arm is sealed around her.

It catches me for second, seeing them all like this.

They're the same people they were last night, all still wearing whatever clothes they'd slept in. But they're exposed in the cold light of day without the firelight painting their faces.

I stuff my hands in my pockets and head down the wooden steps, steeling myself against the wind. Behind me, Brennan summons Javier to the cabin.

I see the look Javier gives Danny when he passes him— the distrust in his eyes, the anger. Danny lowers his gaze in response.

When my path crosses with Javier's, I clap my hand on his shoulder. "Are you okay?" I murmur.

He shakes his head and keeps walking. I hear his sneakers thud up the wooden steps, and the cabin door bangs shut behind him.

My lungs tighten as I join the others at the fir trees.

Eva moves closer to me, and I let her. She threads her fingers through mine.

She gazes up at me with this look of relief, like she's glad that I'm here. Like I'm going to know what to do.

So I hold her hand tighter, and I let her believe it. Because that's just what I do.

Pretend.

Title: Audio File_Javier Ramos Interview

Recording commenced at approximately nine-twenty a.m. on Saturday, April sixteenth. My name is Detective Brennan. Can I take your name, please?

Yeah. Javier Ramos.

I'm sorry for your loss, Javier. I understand you were in a relationship with Piper Meyers. Is that correct?

Yes. (0:25 DELAY) I'm sorry. I need a minute.

That's fine. Take as long as you need.

(2:07 DELAY) Yeah. Yeah, we were together.

How was everything between yourself and Piper last night?

Great. Everything was great with us.

Some of your friends have said that the two of you had been arguing. Why don't you tell me what that was about?

It was nothing. It was me, in my head. We were fine.

Had you been sharing a room with Piper during this trip?

No. Well, yeah. We switched rooms so that Piper and I could spend more time together.

At what point did you realize that Piper hadn't returned to the room last night?

I don't know. I knew she didn't come back, but I thought she was somewhere else. It's my fault, isn't it? I should have gone looking for her. I might have been able to...

Where would she have been last night, if not with you?

(1:03 DELAY) I couldn't trust her. I've been cheated on before. You don't get over something like that easy, you know? I just...

Take your time.

I couldn't trust her. I thought she was lying to me. I started imagining all these things, and then I...

Then you what?

I didn't believe anything she was telling me.

Where were you at around midnight last night, Javier?

I don't know. I was on the beach, getting my head together.

Were you alone?

(0:12 DELAY) No. I was with my friend.

Your friend's name?

Colton.

EVA

I'm in a fog. That's what it feels like. Like I'm trapped in a thick mist, just dimly muddling my way through.

Every time I try to speak, my words seem to come out wrong, scrambled.

The police have finished taking our statements and have asked us all to wait in the communal room. Paul is here making us breakfast and urging us to eat, and helping us clean up the aftermath of last night. It's good to have some stability here, an adult, someone who isn't us. But, honestly, he looks just as shaken and stunned as we do. And beneath his comforting words, I can tell he's horrified that something like this could happen on his property. That *we* let this happen. His eyes keep skating over the empty beer bottles left out on the counter.

Outside, there are a few officers on radios standing at the cordoned off road. Detective Brennan is among them.

Paul talks quietly on his cell in the kitchen as he drops the bottles into the trash with the clink of glass. The rest of us have filled the couches on either side of the fireplace. It's been a while since any of us have spoken.

I stare vacantly at the logs piled up in the hearth. It crosses my mind to light the fire and bring some warmth into the cavernous room. It feels ice-cold in here. Outside, despite the early hour, the sky has darkened, threatening a storm.

From the other side of the low-set coffee table, Alice catches my wandering gaze. "I can't believe this is real," she murmurs to me. Tears glisten in her deep brown eyes. "She was just here…" Her focus moves to the screen door, and the steel gray shoreline beyond.

"I know," I say softly. "Are you okay?"

She shakes her head. "Are you?"

I force myself to look around the group, and my chest tightens. One after another, blank, glazed expressions. Everyone wondering how we ended up here.

I take a small breath. "What happened at the fire last night, after I left?" I whisper to Alice.

There's a beat of silence, then she speaks again. "I don't know." Her gaze wanders over the group. "Miles and I left right after you did." At the mention of his name, Miles's arm knocks against mine as he shifts in his seat. "Piper must have gone off on her own and slipped or something, right?" Alice adds.

"But why would she have been in the cave on her own?" I press, loud enough for the others to start looking our way. "Who would do that?" A memory flashes through my mind. Javier hiding in the shadows of the cave, waiting to jump out on Piper and Alice, and their startled shrieks of laughter rippling across the bay. "Was it a prank gone wrong? Did any-one know she was in there?"

No one responds.

My eyes travel over everyone, and my pulse quickens. The echo of the scream last night still haunts me, the click of stones as someone ran away from the cave, the feel of the shallow pools beneath my shoes.

And the feel of the phone that's still in my pocket, digging into my thigh.

If it was an accident, and if it was Piper's scream that I heard as she slipped in the cave, then why did I hear someone *else* running away?

I hold my voice steady. "Did anyone see Piper leave the fire?"

"Yeah," Karly says quietly. "She left right after Danny did."

Noah clears his throat, and everyone goes quiet.

My mind starts racing in the silence. I can feel Danny tense in the seat beside me, but I can't bring myself to look at him.

Across the room, the front door clicks open, and I flinch. We all turn to stare as Detective Brennan walks into the cabin alongside another officer. His age-lined eyes skate over us in the same careful way that hers do.

Paul strides toward them, his phone still in his hand and the leather case hanging open from his last call. "Hi, Detective Brennan, Detective Mendoza," he greets them. "Can you tell us anything more?"

Their attention moves to the couches, and their eyes land on one person.

Detective Brennan shows her badge as she says the words, "We're going to need to bring you into the station in con-nection with the death of Piper Meyers."

Title: Audio File_Danny Demarco Interview

Hi, Danny. My name is Detective Myra Patel, and it is seven a.m. on Saturday, April sixteenth.

(INAUDIBLE.)

Just take your time, Danny.

(INTERVIEW SUSPENDED FOR 5:25 MINUTES.)

Are you ready to talk me through what happened this morning, Danny?

I found Piper. She was in a cave just down from the place we're staying at. She wasn't moving, I think the tide had come in. Her head was cut…

At what time was this?

It had just started to get light.

So, what, around six a.m.? What were you doing in the cave at that time, Danny?

Looking for Piper. We'd had a fire on the beach last night, our whole group. Piper said she wanted to talk to me, but it didn't happen. I left the fire early, and I waited for her to get back to the rooms, but she didn't show.

What time did everyone else come back from the fire?

Different times. Mostly around midnight, or just after.

If the rest of your friends were back at the accommodation by midnight, why did it take you so long to search for Piper?

I tried looking for her earlier, but it was dark. So, I waited until it started to get light, then I went back out.

Was no one else concerned about Piper's whereabouts? Did any of your friends try to search for her?

I don't know, they didn't seem to notice. She has a boyfriend, Javier, and they've been sharing a room out here. But things weren't good between them.

Why not?

He thought she was cheating on him, but she wasn't.

Okay. Let's rewind to last night. When did you last see Piper alive?

(0:50 DELAY) We were on the beach, all of us. I left because I knew Piper and Javier were fighting because of me, because Piper and I used to date, and it was making things weird, me being on this trip with them. Javier thought I still had feelings for her.

And was Javier right to think that?

No. We were just friends, and she told him that. We both did.

Okay. Were you the first to leave the group last night?

No. Eva, my friend, she left first. Then two of my other friends, Alice and Miles. Then me.

And did you leave alone?

No. I was with my brother, Colton. We left together.

At that time, who remained on the beach?

Piper, Javier, Noah, and Karly.

Okay. Thank you for your cooperation, Danny. We can take a break here. I'll arrange a car to take you back to your accommodations, and I'd like you to stay put at the property for the time being. Would you like to call your parents from the office?

No. Thanks.

COLTON

We're going to need to bring you into the station in connection with the death of Piper Meyers.

My heart feels like it's in my throat. Brennan's eyes pass over me, but then she says another name, not mine.

"Javier Ramos, would you please come with us."

The air falls from my lungs.

Noah's already on his feet, and Eva is, too.

"What?" Javier's voice sounds hoarse. "Me? Why me?"

The two cops are unflinching, casting shadows over the floorboards.

"Whoa." Paul steps forward. "Hold on a second. Why exactly are you questioning him?"

"This isn't an arrest," the older cop, Mendoza, says in a gravelly voice. "But we do need to move this to the precinct. I'd appreciate your cooperation, Mr. Lauder."

Noah looks helplessly at his uncle.

"I didn't do anything." Javier's struggling for his voice, looking quickly between us and the cops. His dark eyes are wide and frantic, jumping from person to person.

"Okay," Paul says, dragging a hand over his jaw. "But I don't want you questioning him until I've spoken to his parents and he has a lawyer."

"We can arrange that," Brennan answers.

"A lawyer?" Javier's breathing fast. "Why do I need a lawyer? I told you I didn't do anything."

"I'll come down to the station, too," Paul says, reaching for his keys.

"Actually, Mr. Lauder," Brennan interrupts, lifting her hand, "we'll need you to stay here with the remaining minors. At least until their parents arrive. I suggest you call them."

Paul's face falls.

"I didn't do anything," Javier rasps again.

My heart slams in my chest, because I realize then, I realize where I've messed up. I was with *Javier*. I said I was with Danny, because it's autopilot, I do it without thinking. It didn't even cross my mind to consider where I *really* was at midnight. Until now. Until the cops are escorting Javier out of the cabin.

I wasn't with Danny; I was with Javier.

I freeze up and panic spikes through me. "Wait." I'm out of my seat fast. "He was with me. He didn't do anything, he was with me."

But the cops barely glance at me. They don't believe me—it's too late.

They lead Javier out through the front door, and Paul grips my shoulder as they leave.

FOUR MONTHS EARLIER

Javier bounds into my English class. He weaves his way through a bunch of empty desks and finds me at the back of the room.

"You're not in this class," I remind him.

English is one of the only classes I actually like, aside from PE and Shop. Unlike Danny, who sails through every subject and has been enrolled in AP classes since sophomore year, English is an exception for me.

Javier pulls up a chair and folds his arms on my desk. "Question for you," he says, seriously. "And it's time-sensitive."

I gesture for him to speak.

"Do you think your brother would mind if I asked Piper out?"

I almost laugh because I think he's joking. But he just looks at me, heavy eyebrows raised, waiting for a response.

I rub my forehead. "Uh, no? I don't know. Ask him."

He falls back in his seat and starts tapping his knuckles on the desk. "You think I should talk to him first? I don't want to cross any bro-code lines." He extends his hands wide. "You know me, Colton. Me and you go way back, I don't want to cause problems with your brother. But him and Piper have been broken up for a while, yeah?"

"I don't know. He doesn't talk to me about it."

Javier scratches his head, knotting his fingers through his grown-out curls. "Ah, it's a tough one. But you know I've always liked Piper, right? Way before she and Danny started dating." He nods, mostly to himself. "I've got a good feeling about this." Then he glances across the room. "Hey, Eva," he calls. She's at the desk two over from me. Her earbuds are in as she sketches in her notebook. Golden brown hair falls in two plaits over her shoulders.

"Eva?" Javier calls a little louder. When she still doesn't respond, he clambers over the empty desks and drops into the seat next to her. She looks up with a start, takes out her left earbud.

She blinks. "Hi," she says, looking surprised. "What's up?"

"Question for you." He grins broadly.

Eva's gaze flickers to me. "Go on," she says to Javier.

I listen from two seats over, half smiling at Javier's enthusiasm.

"Do you think Danny would mind if I asked out Piper Meyers?"

She frowns in the same way I did. She pauses for a second. "I think he'd be okay with it."

Javier gives us both a wide grin. "Yeah. That's what I thought. I've got class with Piper right now. I was going to ask if she wanted to hang out tonight before winter break."

Eva's eyes widen a little and she swaps a smile with me. "Oh," she says, slowly. "Well, good luck. I mean, I hope she says yes."

Javier slaps his hands together and shakes them to the ceiling, then he springs from the seat and pats me on the shoulder as he leaves, calling, "We're still going out to the water this weekend, me, you, and Noah?"

I lift my hand as he heads for the door.

"Wish me luck." He ducks out of the classroom, bumping into the people who are coming in.

I look at Eva and the empty space between us.

She purses her lips and raises her eyebrow. I laugh under my breath and return my attention to my work.

DMEA GROUP CHAT

ALICE: Danny, are you okay? We're all here for you. I'm so sorry about what you went through this morning. I can't imagine.

MILES: Echo that.

EVA: Come find us if you want to talk. I'm so sorry.

DANNY: I know. Thanks.

MILES: This is so surreal. Why did the police take Javier?

DANNY: Because he killed Piper.

EVA

I slip into my room and close the door with a quiet click. My legs feel weak as I lean against the pine wall, just staring numbly at the rain clouds beyond the window. The moody sky is dulling the cove, and the waves are rearing high, crashing against the golden shore.

This can't be real.

I reach for my jeans pocket, feeling the curve of the phone I've been hiding. The reminder that I'm a liar. I lied to the police. I withheld information, evidence.

My stomach rolls at the thought of Piper, and the chilling sound of her scream last night. It must have been her.

I squeeze my eyes shut, breathing slowly as I listen to the groan of the wind outside. Once the police left with Javier, Paul rallied the rest of us, getting us all to call our parents. Everyone's wandering around the property and surrounding beach right now, searching for the best cell service, clutching their phones close to their ears. I tried my parents, but both calls went to voice mail. It didn't seem right to leave them a message or send a text. I wouldn't even know where to start.

Besides, it's not my phone I'm thinking about.

I slide the mystery cell out of my pocket and stare at my faint reflection in the dead, cracked screen. I plug it into the charger on my bedside table—if my suspicion is right, and this really is Piper's phone, I'll know for sure once I see her home screen.

And just like that, I'm right back there, back in the dark cave, my shoes wet from the rising tide and my eyes searching the shadows. Why didn't I notice the ditch? If only I'd have just explored a little farther, I might have found Piper. She must have been so close. If I'd just searched around more, I might have been able to save her. Was she conscious? Did she hear me calling, and worse, was she trying to call back and I just left her there?

Someone knocks on my door, and I jump, almost dropping the phone. "Who is it?" The words come out extra high.

Colton's voice returns to me from the other side. "It's just me. Can I come in?"

With my hands trembling, I twist the door handle. Rain has begun to mist the deck, dampening and darkening Colton's hair, and causing some strands to cling to his brow.

My breath hitches. That feeling of safety just to have him here with me. It's hard to believe that just yesterday him coming into my room would have been the most exciting thing to happen to me, and now everything has a pall over it.

That *should* have been it. Hanging out with Colton should have been the biggest thing to happen last night. Not this.

But here we are, in this screwed up reality that never should have been.

When Colton steps into the room, the door falls closed behind him with a soft thud.

"Are you okay?" he asks, his eyes moving slowly over my face.

"No," I answer, shaking my head. "Are you?"

He doesn't respond. He crosses the room and takes a seat on the edge of my bed. His knee starts bouncing.

Then he looks at me, his deep green eyes meeting mine. "Eva," he murmurs. "I've done something really bad."

EVA

I hold my breath, waiting for Colton to speak.

He locks his broad hands and looks up at me from his seat on the edge of the bed. "I told Brennan I was with Danny all night." He pauses and swallows. "I wasn't."

I press my palm to my heart. "Wait. You really were with Javier? You weren't just saying that?"

"I told Brennan that Danny and I left the fire together, and I was with him at midnight. Because I knew he'd say the same."

"Okay." I hug my arms around myself. "Where were you really?"

"At that time..." He looks down at his sneakers. "I saw you leave the fire, Eva, and I was supposed to follow right after."

I lower my gaze to the floorboards. He was supposed to meet me, but he never showed. I waited up for him, right here in this room, until eventually I fell asleep and woke up to the sound of unfamiliar voices and the flashing lights of police cars.

"I'm sorry," he murmurs, catching my gaze. "I meant to follow. I wanted to."

"It's okay," I tell him. And I mean it. But it *wasn't* okay, at the time. I felt rejected, embarrassed. Considering everything that's happened this morning, though, none of that seems to matter anymore. I'm just glad he's here now.

"Javier started opening up," he carries on, muddling through his thoughts. "About Piper, and how he couldn't trust her. When she and Danny started hanging out again, it got into his head. I don't know exactly what time we left the fire, or what he did after we got back to the rooms, but up until then, I was with him." He holds my stare. "But the cops must have thought I was just trying to cover for Javier. And if I do convince them, it means Danny won't have an alibi. We both lied."

When I speak, my voice sounds small. "Javier not having an alibi can't be their only reason for pulling him in. I was alone last night, too."

"So, they must think they have something more on him."

I don't miss the word *think* in his sentence. Because he doesn't believe it. He doesn't believe that bouncy, happy-go-lucky Javier would kill Piper, would kill anyone. If what happened to Piper wasn't an accident, then whatever evidence the police *think* they have on Javier, surely it's wrong. But I'm not ready to make sense of what that means for the rest of us.

"Or they just wanted to talk to him," I reason. "Like they said."

"But why him? He would never have…" Colton trails off and rubs his brow.

"I know," I say softly. "Javier wouldn't hurt anyone."

His jaw tightens.

When the seconds keep passing us by, I give way to a shaky breath. "Since we're sharing our secrets and all…" I pull the phone from my bedside table, where it's blinked back to life, then hand it to Colton without looking at the screen. I can't bear it yet.

He takes it from me and frowns.

"It's not mine," I explain, taking a seat beside him on the bed. "I think it might be Piper's."

His breathing falters and his shoulders hunch forward.

Now, in the cold light of day, the phone looks too familiar. It's a new model, and I can picture the gold case in Piper's hand as she filmed her Lives in the back seat of Karly's car. Of *course* it was hers all along. I just couldn't admit it to myself, because of what it would mean if it was. Because of what it *does* mean.

My gaze moves to the window where rain has begun to pelt the glass. "When I was waiting for you on the beach last night," I murmur, "I heard someone scream around the cave." I drag my focus back to Colton. He's gnawing on his lip, his stare fixed intently on me, waiting for more. "Given what we know now," I add, "it must have been Piper. I heard someone run away from the cave right after, heading away from the lodge. I called out, but no one answered."

Colton's silent, but his eyes move, shifting between me and the craggy bay beyond the window.

"I told Detective Brennan about the scream," I carry on. "But I didn't tell her about the phone because…" I blow out a breath. "I don't know, I panicked. The way she was leading my answers, I felt like if I told her about the phone, she'd think

I'd taken it. She'd think I had something to hide. Which, I guess, now I do."

He tenses and drags his teeth over his lower lip.

"I had no idea it belonged to Piper at the time." My voice sounds thin. Guilty. "I just figured someone was fooling around and dropped it without realizing."

"Do you know her passcode?" he asks. His eyes linger on the closed bedroom door. It's quiet beyond the room, with only the pattering of rain hitting the deck outside.

Use my phone. Piper's voice echoes in my mind. *Mine's got the best camera.* At the diner, she'd squeezed herself into the spot between Javier and Karly in the booth and started combing her fingers through her glossy hair.

That afternoon, while I propped her phone against the sugar pourer at the end of the table, Piper called out her passcode so that I could unlock the screen.

"I remember it ended with *29*." I chew on my thumbnail. "Her birthday, maybe? She said she was a Scorpio, so October? *10*?"

Colton clears his throat. "Alright. *1029*."

He taps the digits into the phone.

PIPER

ALBUM: SAVED VIDEOS

Hey, dolls! It's Piper. I just wanted to jump on here real quick to show you my looks for spring break. We're leaving in about half an hour so I'm just in the final stages of packing my case, and I wanted to share the chaos with you guys!

As you can see, I have this gorgeous retro pattern halter dress, which I am obsessed with, and this cropped tee. Both are from Candy Blush Boutique. You can use my discount code for 10 percent off your first order. I am in love with these looks, and they're so perfect for my trip to Tillamook County @resortonthewater.

Okay, so, those of you who've been following me for a while will know that my ex, Danny, will be on this trip, too. But, guys, we are all good and there will be no drama. Sorry, loves! Danny and my boyfriend, Javier, are friends, and any bad blood is squashed. Look, I'll hold my hands up and admit that I've talked some shit about Danny in the past, but we've had some heart-to-hearts lately and I truly feel like he is working on himself, which is so good.

Do I entirely trust him? No.

Actually, it's a question I've been asking myself a lot lately. Can you ever really trust anyone, entirely? The answer is no. And that includes me, guys!... Just kidding! You can trust me. Pinky swear.

Anyway, I'll be vlogging the whole trip, so keep checking for my Lives and updates.

Oh, hold on a second...speak of the devil. Danny's literally calling me right now. Okay, I'd better go. Oh, and guys, if you haven't already, go follow my besties Karly, Alice, and Eva. I'll link their handles below so go find them in the comments and follow.

Kiss, kiss. Love you guys.

EVA

An image of Piper posing in front of a pool smiles out at us.

Colton and I are rendered silent by her presence. Her ghost.

I feel him move closer to me, but I can't tear my eyes from the cracked screen and the frozen image of Piper's face.

A painful lump forms in my throat, and I force myself to swallow it away. "The phone was warm," I say, trying to organize my jumbled thoughts. "When I found it in the cave, it was warm, like she'd just used it right before I arrived."

"Here," Colton murmurs, passing the cell to me. "You knew her better than I did. You should look through, see if there's anything that seems off. Last calls, messages, pictures."

I draw in a breath and nod. "Yeah. Okay."

But I stay close to him as I take over control of Piper's phone. There are a few unread texts, nothing that stands out at first glance, and no calls were made or received last night. In Photos, there are tons of saved videos and pictures, and I start working through the recent shots. I don't know what I'm looking for, exactly. I'm just hoping there's something in here that'll help us make sense of this. Make sense of what happened to her.

"Look," Colton says, hovering his finger over the screen as I scroll through the images. "This was on our way here."

I pause on the group shot from the diner. We're all leaning in close in the booth, heads dipped together. Everyone found a pose. Danny's arm is slung over Colton's shoulder, and they're both grinning, their noses crinkling a little. Noah is in a backward ball cap, holding his fingers out like a shotgun. Javier is posing with a goofy smile while he pulls up the sleeve of his T-shirt to expose light brown skin and a flexed bicep. And Miles, only half-visible behind Danny, with his slim arms folded tightly and an awkward, close-lipped smile. At the edge of the frame, Karly, Piper, Alice, and I are huddled together, a mixture of air-kisses and practiced smiles.

Beyond that thumbnail shot, there's row after row of selfies, or pictures of Piper and Javier, with the spiderweb crack splintering their smiles.

In one image, Piper's twisted a strand of hair around her index finger and is blowing a kiss to the camera. Javier's face is pressed close to hers, grinning out from the shattered screen. The cave is a backdrop behind them.

A shiver moves over me, and I move on from the picture. On to last night's amber-streaked faces caught around the fire; mid-laugh, mid-conversation. Danny, Javier, me...

Colton leans closer. "Wait," he says, pointing to one of the pictures. "What's this?" The single image of what looks like a piece of paper stands out in a sea of brightly colored backgrounds and exuberant faces. Judging by its placement in the album, it was taken yesterday.

My heart practically leaps into my throat when I enlarge the shot, because I already know what it is.

Hi Piper,

Ahh, it feels so strange writing you a note like this. But I find it way easier to explain myself on paper. Do you get that?

I know I shut you down pretty bluntly earlier, and the truth is, I do have feelings for someone.

You.

I'm not expecting you to reciprocate. I know you're happy with Javier, and I'm happy for you. But I wanted you to know how I've been feeling because I think it will help you understand the conversation we had, and why I reacted in the way that I did.

Also, I'm a big believer in telling people how great they are. Because it's always good to know, right? I think you're great.

That's all!

EVA

"This has got to be it." My words rush out.

I drag my gaze to Colton, but his stare is still fixed on the image displayed on Piper's phone. The photo taken of a handwritten note—*the* handwritten note—is now enlarged on Piper's cracked screen. "This has to be the letter Javier found." The picture captures the creases and folds in the page from where it was balled in Javier's fist.

Colton takes a slow breath.

"But that…" I point to the screen, where the neatly written words spill down the notepaper. "That's not Danny's handwriting." My stomach flips and I struggle to keep my voice even, not to blurt out right away whose handwriting I *think* this is. "Danny lied to us. He didn't write that. But why would he say he did?"

Colton's eyes wander to the closed door, as though he's half expecting someone to burst in on us at any moment, and find us in here, harboring Piper's missing phone. My pulse quickens at the thought.

"Okay." Colton works his lip between his teeth. "Piper's got to have known that this wasn't from Danny," he says. "They dated for months. She must have known that this isn't his writing."

"Well, yeah. Danny used to pass notes to her in class all the time back then."

"And right here," he says, gesturing to the last few lines of the note. "*I wanted you to know how I've been feeling because I think it will help you understand the conversation we had, and why I reacted in the way that I did,*" he reads aloud. "Piper would have known who she'd had that conversation with."

My heart is racing. I can't bring myself to look at him. "Okay, so maybe she was protecting the identity of whoever did write it," I say quietly.

"Who do you think it was?"

When I don't answer, he speaks again.

"Well, whoever it was, they let Danny take the heat for it," he says, grimacing. "They let Javier think it was him. They let us all think it was him."

His focus moves back to the phone, and he scrolls through more rows of images and videos. He stops at the last thumbnail—a video taken last night. The pitch-black background is the final bookend in a long assortment of pictures taken around the fire, where everyone's faces are only lit in part, and amber flames are curling in the background.

"Piper took this video at..." Colton leans a little closer to read the time stamp. He breathes sharply, and I freeze when I realize what he's seen.

"Just after midnight." My voice fails me, barely a whisper.

In the center of the black background, a white arrow stands out. Holding my breath, I tap on the Play symbol.

Suddenly, the video fills the entire screen. There's movement, but it's impossible to see anything clearly; it's too dark. Piper's voice jumps out into the room. She's breathless. Angry.

"You think you can threaten me? I'm done with this. I'm going to tell everyone what you did—"

The image jolts in the darkness, and the bloodcurdling sound of Piper's scream concludes the video.

COLTON

I'm going to tell everyone what you did. Her words haunt the room.

People always ask us, Danny and me, if we can read each other's minds because we're twins.

We can't.

But at times like this I wish we could.

I swallow the tightness building inside my chest. Eva's hand brushes mine. I don't know if she meant to do it, but I'm glad that she did. That touch jolts me from wherever my head was spiraling toward.

"Someone was threatening Piper," she says, breathing fast. "She had something over them." The way Eva looks at me, straight into my eyes, full of fear, it makes me flinch. Then she says, "One of us. Someone here was threatening Piper, and then they killed her."

My eyes stray to the door, and the wall that divides us and

the others. Rain hammers on the roof and streams down the windowpanes.

"Does anyone else know you've got this phone?" My voice sounds ragged.

She shakes her head. She's nervous, scratching at her hands. "I asked around to see if anyone had lost their phone last night, but at that point I didn't realize it was Piper's."

"Alright. Whoever was with her in the cave might not know she'd been trying to record them. They probably don't know she dropped her phone, otherwise they would have picked it up themselves, right?"

"That would make sense," she agrees. "After I heard the scream last night, I heard someone run away. Maybe they panicked when she fell, and they just got out of there fast." She presses her fingertips to her eyelids. "I can't believe this is real," she murmurs. "I don't want this to be real."

I fold my arm around her, and she leans into me, resting her head on my shoulder. It feels more natural than it should, but we both need comfort right now. We need each other.

"Last night at the fire," she says, quietly. "After I left, what happened?"

I stare at the window and the rain spilling down the glass. "Alice and Miles took off after you," I answer, piecing it together from what I can remember. "I went with Javier to get more wood for the fire, and that's when we ended up talking for a while. Away from the others."

She sits up straighter to look at me. "What did Javier say about Piper?"

"Only that he cared about her a lot, and he wanted to fix things. He wasn't mad at her, but he didn't know if he could trust her. That note got into his head. Danny got into his head."

Eva nods slowly. "So, he didn't seem angry, exactly?"

"Not angry enough to kill her, if that's what you're thinking."

Her gaze drops to the floor. "I didn't mean… I didn't think that…"

"I know," I say, drawing her eyes back to mine. "I get it. Anyway, I told Javier that Danny wasn't interested in Piper anymore, but I know he didn't believe me. And now that I've read that note, I get why."

"Well, if he thought Danny wrote those things to Piper…" she trails off.

"By the time we got back to the fire, Danny was gone. So was Piper."

Eva laughs under her breath, but there's no humor to it. "Oh, great. Hardly reassuring for Javier."

"Yeah," I mutter. "Karly and Noah were still there. Apparently, Piper had gone looking for Javier a couple of minutes before we got back, so he went to go find her."

"But he ended up coming back to the rooms alone."

"According to Danny."

"What time did Javier go looking for Piper?" she asks.

"I don't know. But it must have been after midnight. Maybe half past."

"So, the only people who were technically alone at *that* time were Javier, Piper, Danny, and me…"

"And me," I add. "Because I left right after Javier. And Karly and Noah, or Alice and Miles, too, if either of those pairs split up at any point."

Eva heaves a sigh. "Great. So, that narrows it down to all of us."

"All of us," I agree.

She holds my stare, and my heart thumps in my chest. Now she knows the truth. If she shares this with the cops, or anyone, then I've just blown up my own alibi. And Danny's.

But it's not just me who's taken a leap of faith. Eva told me about Piper's phone. She didn't have to. Even if I'd seen her with it, I'd never have guessed that it belonged to Piper.

I told her my lie, and she told me hers. We're in this together now.

And if I'm going to put my trust in anyone, it'd always be her. Eva was that kid in elementary school who'd ask her mom to give us a ride home from school when our own mom forgot to show. She'd do it subtly, acting like it was no big deal when we made up some weak excuse about Mom's car being in the shop. But I knew she knew. She'd always invite us to her parties, too, even though back then our clothes never fit right and always had a couple of holes or rips. She never judged us or made us feel less than her. She never labeled us as the bad kids.

I trusted her back then, and I still trust her now.

We both jolt as the door handle twists.

Karly steps into the room and closes the door behind her. Her eyes are smudged black and tear tracks are marking her cheeks. She notices me sitting beside Eva on the bed, and she falters. It only takes a second for her to shake it off and continue to her side of the room, but I saw it, that look she gave me. She crawls onto the other bed and hugs a pillow to her chest. "My mom's driving out today," she says to us.

Eva inhales slowly. "That's good. I should try calling my parents again."

Karly starts fiddling with the corner of a pillowcase. She's blinking fast, like she's trying not to cry.

"Are you okay?" I ask. I cringe as I say it because anyone can see she's a long way from okay.

She doesn't respond. She doesn't look at me.

I stand from Eva's bed. "I'm going to go."

When I start for the door, Karly mutters something under her breath. I swear I hear the words...*back to Danny*. I stop at the door, gripping the brass handle. "Are we good, Karly?"

She hugs the pillow tighter and brings her gaze to me. "Yeah, of course. I just..." She gives way to a small breath, swiping at a tear as it rolls down her cheek. "I just can't believe Javier killed Piper."

The ways she says it, though. It's not that she can't believe it—it's that she *doesn't* believe it.

THREE MONTHS EARLIER

"Let's do this." Javier slaps his hands together.

I stare down at the gray water fifty feet beneath us as it surges and churns. The sun is just rising, and it's cold out this morning, well into winter. The icy wind bites.

Our legs hang over the precipice. Javier, Noah, and me, sitting side by side on the cliff edge, shoulder to shoulder. Ready to jump.

"Okay," Noah says, shaking out his arms. "Okay. Let's go." He hesitates and looks left to right, glancing at both of us. "Unless we for real just go. Home."

Javier laughs and smacks his arm. "Don't be saying shit like that, man." The wind tosses around his jet-black curls. "This is living. This is the moment."

Noah pulls his jacket tighter. "It's goddamn freezing up here."

I look over his head, catching Javier's eye and grinning. "You're about to get a lot colder down there," I say to Noah. I rub my hands together for warmth as the wind whips at our hair and clothes.

"You all suck," Noah says, puffing a fogged breath into the air. "Next year, I'm out."

Javier grips his shoulder. "What?" His smile is wide. "You can't be out. This is tradition! There is no out."

"It's the worst tradition ever," Noah grunts. "We're lucky we haven't gotten hypothermia. Or broken our necks."

I look down at the water below, gray and frothing as it slaps the rock wall. "Wasn't this your idea to start with?"

Noah snorts and rakes his hands through his shaggy hair. "Yeah. But I was, like, twelve years old. I didn't know about hypothermia and broken necks back then."

Javier keeps a grip on his shoulder, still smiling big. "Noah, man. This is tra-di-tion, and we're keeping it going until we're old men smoking on our pipes up here." He props a cigarette into Noah's mouth and sparks up the end, shading the lighter's flame from the wind.

"We might not even be here next year," Noah says in a breath of smoke.

We all look down at the snapping jaws of the water.

Then Noah clears his throat. "I mean, college and all that. We're all going to different places. We might not be home for winter break."

Javier's mouth falls open. "Have you heard this guy?" he says, leaning forward to talk to me over Noah. "Not even finished the year yet and he's already planning on dropping us for his shiny new college

*buddies. Last year he was all for blowing off college, and this year he's
an A-student, not even coming back for winter break."*

Noah laughs and shoves Javier's shoulder. *"Yeah, well, maybe my
shiny new college buddies won't make me jump off cliffs."*

Javier grins and holds up his palms. *"Hey, man. Ain't nobody
forcing nobody. This is your own free will."*

"Speaking of free will," I say to Javier. *"Have you told Piper
you're not applying to LA with her yet?"*

"No way," he says, shuddering. *"She'll lose it. She's already got
our whole year planned out."*

Noah grins. *"Good luck with that. If this jump doesn't kill you,
she will."*

"Anyway," Javier says, *"I'm thinking it'd make life easier if I just
go with her. I want to be with Piper, so…"*

I frown back at him. *"Are you sure? What if you guys break up?
Then you're stuck with her plans instead of your own."*

"We're not going to break up. I love her." He says it with such
conviction that I almost laugh.

"Already? You've only been together for a couple of weeks."

"Yeah, but I just know," he says, pressing his fist to his heart.
*"She's the one for me, I'm telling you. And if I have to go along with
some stuff to make it work, I will. It's called compromise, man. I'll do
what I've got to do."* He looks between us, seriously. *"Noah, what
was it your uncle told us? Go hard for what you want."*

"Yup," Noah says.

"So I'll do whatever it takes."

I toss a pebble over the edge, and we all watch as the water swallows
it. *"Alright."* I stand and brush the dirt from my hands. *"For what
might be the last time, let's do this."* I start walking away from the
precipice. I hear the crunch of earth behind me as they do the same.

But I don't look to see if they've followed because I know that they have. I close my eyes and sprint back to the edge.

"Sink or swim, boys!" Javier calls.

My sneakers leave the ground, and I'm falling through the air.

The ice-cold water envelops me.

EVA

When the door clicks shut behind Colton, I cross the room and join Karly on her bed. "How are you holding up?"

She dabs at her eyes with her sleeve. Strands of hair are clinging to her damp cheeks. "Not good," she whispers. "You?"

"Not good, either," I murmur.

"Piper," she says, and her voice catches. "I can't believe this. I can't believe Javier..." She ends the sentence with a fractured breath. "Do you think that's why the police took him? Because they think that he..."

I shake my head. "Honestly, I don't know. It doesn't—"

A knock on the door makes us both stop. I look at Karly, and she nods.

"Come in," I call.

The handle twists and the door opens. Alice ducks into the room, shying away from the rain sweeping across the deck. She pushes the door closed behind her, trapping the wind outside. But the flurry of cold air still makes me shiver.

"Hi," I manage.

She musters a weak smile. Without a word, she crosses the room to join us on the bed. I shuffle closer and pull her into a hug. When we break apart, Alice's eyes rove over Karly's tearstained cheeks. "I'm sorry," she whispers, reaching out to take her hand.

"Yeah," Karly answers, gently squeezing Alice's fingers in response. "Me, too."

"I just got off the phone with my parents," Alice says. "They're going to come here today."

"Mine, too," Karly tells her.

"Javier..." Alice folds her arms around herself. "I mean..." She exhales in a long breath. "We were with him this morning, freaking out, everyone wondering what was going on, and he acted as clueless as the rest of us. I just can't wrap my head around this."

Karly holds her pillow tighter.

"Let's not jump to conclusions," I reason quietly. "Just because the police have taken Javier into the station, it doesn't mean that he had anything to do with what happened to Piper. They only wanted to talk to him."

"But if he did," Alice says, meeting my gaze, "that means that he stood there this morning and lied to all of our faces. Knowing..." she trails off and swallows.

My eyes are drawn across the room to my bed and the corner of Piper's cell just visible beneath the comforter. A wave of guilt flips my stomach. I'm the fraud. I'm the liar.

"Guys." I hear the tremor in my voice, but I can't back

out. Between the scream and footsteps I heard last night and the incriminatory video on Piper's phone, it's looking likely that someone in our group killed Piper. The three of us, we can't afford to lie to each other. If I want them to be honest with me, I need to be honest with them. I need to make the call on who I can trust, and who I can't. And I trust them. I hope. "There's something you should know."

Both their stares are immediately on me. They're sitting straighter now, holding their breath.

"What?" Karly presses.

I stand, weakly, and walk to my side of the room. As they watch, I retrieve the phone that I'd slipped beneath the blanket when Karly walked in.

The confused expressions on their faces last a couple of seconds. Then Karly draws in a small breath. "Where did you get that?"

"I found it in the cave, right after I heard Piper scream."

Karly stares steadily at me, and Alice's brow crinkles.

"Wait, what?" Alice says. "Whose phone is that?"

I type in the passcode and scroll to the last video Piper filmed. Bracing myself, I hit Play.

You think you can threaten me? I'm done with this. I'm telling everyone what you did—

Alice sucks in a sharp breath. "*What?*"

Karly presses her hands to her mouth. Tears begin to spill down her cheeks. "I don't want to hear this," she rasps. "I can't."

I exit the video and set the phone down on the nightstand. Through its splintered face, Piper's background image—the selfie in front of a pool—smiles at us until it fades to black.

"Javier?" Alice asks, looking quickly between us. "Piper knew what he did? What did he do?"

"Or..." My pulse starts to race as I prepare to say the words. "If it wasn't Javier, then who?" Wind rattles the windowpanes, and rain pelts the glass.

Something shifts, then. The way in which they're looking at me. The way Alice sits straighter, and Karly shrinks away from me.

My stomach plummets as the thought hits me. What have I just done?

"How did you say you found this phone?" Karly asks in a trembling voice.

A bolt of fear shoots through me. "Okay, I know it looks bad," I say, holding up my hands. "But I promise you, I found it in the cave. I didn't see anything. It was dark and—"

I don't get to finish my sentence because I'm interrupted by someone pounding on the door.

EVA

"I'm coming in, okay?" Danny's voice reaches us from the corridor.

I quickly plug Piper's phone into the charger and slip it out of sight. Given the way Alice and Karly responded to my admission, I'm not sure I'm ready to include Danny into this conversation, too. Not yet, anyway.

The door swings open, and he stands in the threshold, still gripping the handle. His dark hair is drenched, and the shoulders of his T-shirt are spattered with rain. There's a hardness to his expression, his jaw tight, and his eyes narrowed. "Eva," he says. "We need to talk. Right now."

Blood rushes to my head as I look between Alice and Karly. I turn back to Danny where he waits in the doorway, letting in a stream of cold air. "We're kind of in the middle of something."

"Eva," he says again. His eyes are fixed only on me, conveying something I can't understand. "For real. I need to talk to you." He glances toward the outer corridor, where the growing gale is sweeping sheets of rain through the wooden structure.

"Can it wait?"

He shakes his head. "No."

With a resigned sigh, I climb off the bed. I give Karly and Alice one last look as I leave the room, hoping that they still trust me. They frown back at me, their brows furrowed in confusion. Perfect. Between Piper's phone, and Danny's secretive we-need-to-talk outburst, I can only imagine what they're thinking.

Alice is my best friend, but right now, the way she's looking at me, the way she's leaning closer to Karly, I feel like a total stranger.

"I'll be right back," I tell them hoarsely.

I jostle Danny into the corridor and close the door after us. "You have the worst timing," I say under my breath. "I was in the middle of trying to *not* look like a murderer."

"Do it later." He starts for his room, and I cross my arms tightly as I follow him. Rain lashes against the slanted roof above the deck, drowning out the sound of the ocean. Across the clearing, the trees are bowing to the wind and their branches are groaning and cracking. Danny herds me into his room and shuts the door.

I stop in my tracks, standing still in the little room. Colton is seated on his bed with his hands locked. He looks up at me and shakes his head, mouthing, "Sorry."

"Eva," Danny says, raking his hands through his hair and pushing back the wet strands. "You need to listen and trust me when I tell you this." He stands before me, stooping to meet my eyes. "You need to get rid of that phone."

My mouth falls open and I look at Colton. "You told him?"

Colton rubs his brow. "I had to," he says, wincing. "I told him about the picture of the note, and that I knew he didn't write it—"

"Yeah, he told me," Danny interrupts, breathing fast. "And it's lucky for you that he did. I'm about to save your ass."

I keep my arms tightly crossed. "I'm not getting rid of the phone, Danny. It's evidence in Piper's *murder* investigation."

He drags his hands down his face. "Eva. Please. Listen to me. If the cops find out you've been hiding that phone, they're going to be all over you. They're going to think you did it."

I steal another glance at Colton, but he's looking at the floor now.

Straightening, I return my attention to Danny. "I can't get rid of it, that's not an option. I'll just have to explain that I found it and didn't realize it was Piper's until this morning. Which is true."

Danny throws up his arms. "Oh, yeah. Because that doesn't sound sketchy *at all.*"

I keep my expression cool, even though I'm spiraling on the inside. Because he's right. This is exactly why I didn't tell the police about the phone in the first place—because it makes me look guilty. It'll look even worse now that I *forgot* to mention it when I was being interviewed this morning. I saw the way Karly's and Alice's faces changed when they found out I'd been hiding Piper's phone. They're my friends, I trusted them with this secret, and even they were suspicious of me. *Alice*, the person I share *all* my secrets with, is suspicious of me.

"Give me the phone," Danny says, steadily. "I'll get rid of it for you. It'll be like it never happened." He extends his hand, waiting.

I squeeze my eyes shut and massage my temples. "I need some time to think this through."

In the silence, I hear Piper's voice in my mind. The echo of her final words caught on video. The thought of the phone slipping from her fingers as she fell. Or worse, was pushed.

"Don't worry," Colton murmurs. "You don't have to get rid of it if you don't want to."

But Danny chokes out a sound. "Come on, Colton. You know this looks bad. If anyone else finds out—"

"I've already told Karly and Alice," I say weakly.

Danny slaps his forehead. "You told *Karly*? Why, Eva?"

"Because I didn't want to lie to my friends! They're grieving, and they're confused. We all are."

He heaves a sigh.

"I could tell the police I found the phone in the lodge, this afternoon," I say quickly.

"Yeah," Danny answers. "And do you trust everyone here to keep your secret? Even if Karly and Alice go along with it, I was on the deck last night when you were asking people if they'd lost a phone. It only takes one person to mention that to the cops, then they'll put two and two together and figure out that you *took* the phone from the cave, and then you lied about it."

I look at the window, out to the cove and rocky shoreline. The ocean is wild, crashing and shattering against the shore. Everything is misted by the rain, but the mouth of the cave is just visible.

I'm going to tell everyone what you did.

The echo of Piper's scream tremors through me. I wince and fold my arms around myself.

"I just need some time to think."

But Danny's right. I can't get away from this. None of us can.

COLTON

When Eva leaves our room, I give her a look, a nod. I know she sees it, and I hope it reminds her that I'm here for her, with her. We're still in this together.

But she disappears onto the deck and closes the door behind her.

Danny slumps on his bed. "Thanks for backing me up," he says, tossing a pillow at me.

I catch it and frown. "We can't force her to get rid of the phone if she doesn't want to. Anyway, she's right, it's evidence."

His eyes narrow. For a second, I see the same expression my mom gives when things don't go her way. The frustration that furrows her brow—and his—because it never occurs to them that their plans have holes. "But you know she can't keep it," he says. "She can't get caught with it."

"The cops will be looking for that phone, regardless. Eva could just leave it lying around somewhere."

He grimaces. "With yours and Eva's fingerprints all over it. Smart plan."

"We could wipe it clean."

"Yeah," he says, "and that's all good as long as Karly or someone doesn't drop the real story."

My eyes stray to the window—the same window that Eva had stared out of just minutes earlier. She was scared, and there was nothing I could say or do to change that. It's spreading through all of us, making us act in ways we shouldn't be.

"I hear you," I say, turning back to Danny. "But too many people know about it now to just get rid of it. That could end up looking worse for Eva. Anyway, there might be something on it that clears Javier's name."

Danny laughs.

When I raise an eyebrow, he shakes his head and his jaw clenches.

"What?"

"Just because Javier's your friend, doesn't mean he's innocent."

I hold his stare. "What makes you think he isn't?"

"The cops had reason to pull him in," he elaborates, "they must have."

"Because he didn't have an alibi," I shoot back. "Neither did you."

"And neither did you. You weren't with Javier the whole night. You don't even know what time you got back here, so how can you be sure you were with him at the time Eva *thinks* she heard a scream?"

I don't respond.

The muscles in his jaw twitch. "Javier killed Piper," he says. Then he slaps his hand to his chest. "And I'm not letting my friend, my *innocent* friend, take the fall for it just because she found some phone."

"That's not fair," I mutter. "I care about Eva, too. The cops aren't even looking at her as a suspect."

"But they will."

I rub the nape of my neck.

"So, maybe we should take the phone," he says. "Then it's out of her hands."

I trap my lip between my teeth and look down at my sneakers and the scuff marks on the toes. "We're not taking the phone. We've got to think it through better than that."

EVA

Alice steps out of my room at the same time I leave Colton and Danny's—only, she doesn't seem to notice me. Strands of her dark hair have come free from her long braid and are fluttering in the wind. She lets the door fall shut behind her, and begins moving down the corridor, heading away from me.

I rush to catch up with her, stepping over branches that have been swept into the corridor by the gale. Alice startles when I grasp her arm.

"Hey, what did—"

I press my finger to my lips, and nod farther along the corridor, past Danny and Colton's room, to the side of the building.

She frowns but follows me as I pace quickly around the lodge, over the planked deck and down the stone steps that lead to the cove.

Rain has hardened the sand and misted the salty air. Alice and I stay close to the rocky wall that binds the bay, but we can't hide from the storm as it whips at our hair and clothes. We're alone on the stretch of sand beneath the lodge, far enough away to go unnoticed. The cave is lost behind fog, but the crash of waves sounds louder than ever.

"What's wrong?" Alice asks, squinting in the wet gale. "What did Danny say to you?"

I glance back at the lodge, making sure that we're truly alone. The windows reflect black, and it's hard to tell if anyone's beyond the panes, watching us. I take a quick breath and return my focus to Alice. "I'm just going to come right out with this."

She frowns. "Okay. Sounds ominous."

"I know it was you."

Her breath falters, and I know that I'm right.

Title: Audio File_Alice Moloi Interview

Good morning. My name is Detective Brennan, and the time is approximately ten a.m. on April sixteenth. Can I take your name, please?

Alice Moloi.

Thanks, Alice. Why don't you talk me through what happened here last night.

I don't know. We were all on the beach for a while, then we went back to our rooms. I went to bed a little after one and woke up to this. It's so much to process. I can't wrap my head around it, honestly.

I understand. Alice, how was the mood amongst your friends last night? Some of your group have mentioned that Piper had a disagreement with her boyfriend.

Yes. Yes, that's right. But it was just trivial stuff, I think. It wasn't over anything big.

What were they arguing about?

I don't know. Nothing, really. Or maybe just small stuff.

Okay. And how about yourself, what time did you leave the beach last night?

I'm not sure, exactly. A little before midnight.

Did you leave alone?

No, I was with my friend Miles.

But you and Miles left ahead of the rest of the group? Why was that?

Actually, we were looking for our friend Eva. She left just before us, so we thought we'd catch up with her back at the lodge.

And did you go straight back to the accommodation after you left the fire?

Pretty much.

Can you elaborate on that, please?

Yes. Um. We sat on the beach for a little while, away from the others so that we could talk.

What was it that you needed to talk privately about, if you don't mind me asking?

Oh. Nothing in particular.

You were talking about nothing? That seems strange, considering you stepped away from your friends so that you could talk alone.

No, but... That wasn't why we left the others. We were following Eva, and...and then we just started talking. Just about life, and our plans for next year. Miles really wanted to go to Harvard, but it didn't work out, so he's been feeling pretty down about it.

Okay. Alice, I'm going to ask you something, and I hope you'll give me an honest answer. Do you think your friend Javier had reason to harm his girlfriend, Piper?

No. No, not at all. Okay, they were fighting, but it was nothing. It was all a misunderstanding, and it certainly wasn't Piper's fault. It wasn't anyone's fault.

EVA

"I recognized your handwriting."

When I say the words, Alice closes her eyes. Her shoulders drop.

"Danny didn't write that note to Piper," I hedge. "You did. Piper took a picture of the note on her phone, and I recognized your handwriting, Alice."

She presses the heels of her hands to her brow.

"Everyone thinks it was Danny," I say. "Even Danny thinks it was him!"

Alice musters a thin smile. "Yeah, well. That isn't exactly true."

I brace against the cold and damp wind. "Wait, what do you mean? Does Danny know?"

"Of course he knows, Eva." She drops her hands. "When that fight happened between Danny and Javier, I told Danny right away. I was going to tell Javier, too. I wanted to. But Danny stopped me."

I shake my head, confused. "Why?"

She heaves a sigh. "Eva, you and I are best friends, right?"

"Of course. Always."

"And you know I tell you everything."

"Yeah." I reach for her hand. "Same."

Her eyes wander away from me and her gaze lands on the sullen shoreline. "But I wasn't ready for everyone to know about my feelings for Piper, and when I was honest with Danny about the note, we talked, and he told me not to say anything. The fight was already done and over, that's what Danny said. He said it didn't matter if people thought it was him, and that this would buy me some time to speak to Piper privately, without everyone else getting involved." She brings her eyes back to me, and I notice the glassiness with tears threatening to spill. She shakes off the emotion and inhales sharply. "But I never got a chance to talk to Piper."

"Right," I murmur.

She sweeps aside the strands of her hair that are being tossed around by the wind. "I know I should be honest with everyone, but they're going to wonder why I didn't say anything sooner. I just feel like the worst person ever." She takes another fractured breath and rubs roughly at her eyes with the sleeve of her sweatshirt.

"Alice…"

"I only wrote that note because of how badly the conversation ended when we were all in your room the other night. Piper and I had been getting on so great. As friends," she clarifies, holding up her hands. "But she kept asking me who I was interested in, suggesting she could set me up with Noah, and I panicked. I snapped at her, and I felt awful about it."

"I had no idea you felt this way," I say, searching her eyes. "I'm sorry."

"I never expected Piper to reciprocate," she adds, blotting a tear from the corner of her eye. "I wasn't trying to steal her away from Javier or anything like that. I just wanted to be transparent with her. And then when Javier found the note, I guess he assumed it was from Danny because of their history and..." She squeezes her eyes shut. "Danny and I just figured it'd blow over."

"But it didn't."

She works her lip between her teeth and gazes down at the sand. Our shoes are sinking into the wet ground, spattered with the dark grains. "Do you think I should tell the police about the note?" she asks. "I don't want people using this as a reason to suspect Danny for...for what happened to Piper," she finishes quietly.

I don't answer. Because how am I supposed to advise her on this? After all, I'm hardly in a position to preach about what people should and shouldn't share with the investigators.

"This gives me motive to harm Piper, that's what people will think." She avoids my gaze when she says it. Her eyes wander to the misted cave. Alongside it, the ocean rears and crashes against the shore.

I catch my hair as the wind spirals it. "Miles was with you last night. That counts for something. You guys were together at the time Piper fell."

"Actually." She takes a small breath. "We weren't."

A shiver crawls down my spine, and the wind howls.

"We were looking for you," she explains, glancing back at the lodge. The bleak sky seems to be closing in on it, darkening the log walls in shadow. Alice lowers her voice. "Miles and I separated for a little bit. But I didn't tell the police that. Neither did Miles."

"Okay," I say slowly.

My thoughts start racing. If that final video taken on Piper's phone is anything to go off, someone among us did push her. Piper was threatening someone, and they snapped. I saw the way Alice and Karly looked at me when I showed them the phone. If they considered me, should I be considering them?

It takes me a while to find my voice. "Why Piper?"

Her gaze drifts to the bleak horizon. "There was just something," she murmurs. "Her energy, her enthusiasm, her confidence…" She gives way to a quiet breath. "The way she made me feel like I was important. Like I mattered."

"Of course you matter, Alice," I whisper.

She bows her head. "I liked being around her," she says softly. "I'm going to miss her so much, Eva."

I thread my fingers through hers. "I know," I tell her gently.

Of course, I get it, the appeal. Piper had a magnetic way of drawing people in.

But she had an unparalleled way of pushing people out, too.

GIRLS GROUP CHAT

KARLY: Eva, what happened with Danny? Where are you? I don't want to be on my own, I'm in the communal room and don't know what to do. Paul is making food, but I can't eat.

EVA: Hang in there. I'm going to try calling my parents again and then I'll come find you.

KARLY: Alice, where are you?? I need you. I'm not doing so great.

ALICE: I've been outside. I'm going to go dry off and change, but then I promise I'll stay with you, okay?

KARLY: Okay. Hurry.

COLTON

The storm bats at the windows, shaking the glass. It's getting bad out there, and the roof is leaking, steadily dripping rainwater onto the floorboards.

Danny is lying on his bed, staring up at the ceiling. Miles is sitting on the floor across the room, leaning against the wall. His hands are twitching, thumbs constantly moving. The dark clouds have dimmed the day, losing us in shadows.

I check my phone. No service.

"We should call Mom." I don't look at Danny when I say it, but I hear his bed creak as he sits up.

"Is that a joke?"

I frown at him. "Do I sound like I'm joking?"

"We can't call Mom," he says, shaking his head. "If she gets involved, it'll just make everything worse. You know what she's like, she'll overreact."

"Overreact?" I echo. "Danny, we're in a murder investigation."

"*We're* not," he says. "Javier is."

"She's going to be wondering what's going on."

I notice Miles's gaze drift between us, and it makes me wonder how much Danny has shared with him about my mom and his volatile relationship with her. We don't usually talk about this stuff outside the two of us.

"She won't even know," Danny says. "We said we'd be home on the *weekend* and it's only Saturday. The cops will probably let us go home tomorrow."

Miles looks at me from across the room and raises an eyebrow.

I get why Danny doesn't want to call home. Things have been bad lately, for all of us. Danny blew up at Mom right before we left, called her out on a couple of things. I backed him because I always do. I told her I thought she was selfish, and she sucked in her cheeks like she'd been slapped. Normally, I don't talk back to my mom, and I think that's why it got to her more than when Danny was firing off. I'm supposed to be the levelheaded one, the dependable one who always keeps his shit together, takes care of everyone. But I hit my limit that day. It'd been brewing for a while, months, all three of us swallowing down our true feelings, and then the night before we left, Danny broke, and we all fell with him.

I rub my eyes with the heels of my hands. "We're going to have to tell her what's going on. Someone died, Danny."

He reclines on the bed and stares up at the ceiling. "Yeah, I know, Colton. Piper. Piper died." I hear the catch in his voice.

Across the room, Miles shifts, crossing his legs. "You don't have to remind us of that, Danny," he says, an edge in his voice. "We all know it already. You're not the only one affected by this."

Danny frowns at him.

"And your brother's right," Miles adds. "You need to tell your mom. This is going to come out. It's probably all over the news in Seattle by now. My parents have already spoken to Alice's family about arranging travel down here. Someone's probably contacted your mom by now, too. She's probably worried, trying to call you and not getting through."

"You don't know my mom," Danny scoffs. He keeps his attention on the wood-planked ceiling. "Anyway, it's got nothing to do with us," he says under his breath. "Javier's the one who's been arrested, not us."

Miles starts rocking back and forth.

"Danny…" I try again.

His eyes snap to me. "I already told you, I'm not calling home. Look, no one's stopping *you* from doing it, just don't expect her to show up for you. And don't expect me to talk to her. I'm done with it."

Another raindrop drips from the ceiling, smacking onto the floorboards.

Miles flinches, and I run my hand over my brow.

"Okay," I mutter.

SEVEN MONTHS EARLIER

"Hey, Mom." It's nearly midnight. The kitchen is dark with just a weak lamp glowing on the table. "You're still awake?" She's seated at the folding table with her glasses pushed up into her wild brown

hair. Bills and paperwork are spread out chaotically in front of her. Never a good sight.

"Oh, Colton." She pinches the bridge of her nose and blinks the tiredness from her eyes. "You're home late."

"Yeah. I've been at Javier's place. Is everything okay?" I take a glass from the cupboard and fill it from the faucet. Pots and pans have piled up around the sink. I've been meaning to clean them, but I've been working back-to-back shifts at Summits this weekend.

"We're overdue on rent," Mom mumbles, picking at her bitten-down fingernail. She pushes the paperwork away.

"Don't worry." I lean against the counter and drain my glass. "I can help. I get paid this week."

"Okay. I just…" Her hands are shaking, I see it now in the low light. "I don't know how it got away from me this month. Maybe my check bounced. Maybe…" She looks at me, and I know right away. I know it's worse.

"What's going on?"

She presses her trembling hands together and draws them to her mouth. "I got fired."

My heart slams in my chest. "Oh. Okay. Well, you'll find something else."

"I'm trying," she says, and her gaze wanders away from me to the dusty cloth lampshade. "It's been a couple of weeks. Or longer," she adds quietly.

Pulling out a chair opposite, I join her at the table. "It'll be okay, don't worry." I drum my knuckles on the table. "Danny and I can cover bills this month. I can take on extra shifts while you get back on your feet." As the words come out, my stomach tightens. I don't know how I'll fit in any more shifts between what I'm already doing and school. My grades have already dropped, even after I swore to my grandparents that I'd keep my GPA up. But I've got to earn money, and seeing Mom struggling like this, looking sick, and keeping all the lights out just to save on electricity, it doesn't feel like I've got much choice. I'll make it work.

Then her eyes move away from me, and a tear rolls down her cheek. "I thought I could make it back, and it...it just got out of hand, Colton. I'm so sorry."

My eyebrows pull together. "What do you mean? What got out of hand?"

"The money," she whispers.

"What money?"

"The money from Eileen and Silas."

And then it hits me, slams me in the rib cage. With those few words, my future slips out of my reach. I can't speak.

"I thought it was a sure thing," she murmurs, tears streaming down her face.

No words leave me. Nothing.

"Say something?" she pleads, reaching for my hand across the table.

I pull back. "You gambled our college fund away?"

She presses her hand to her mouth and chokes out a sob through her fingers.

"It's all gone?" I ask.

She nods, shakily.

It takes me a moment to figure it out, to work out what that means. For me. For Danny.

"We've got all year." My voice sounds thin. "We need to start saving. Danny should still go to college. Me and you, we'll figure it out."

She falters. "Do you think we'll be able to save enough to cover Danny's fees?" she whispers.

"We can try. We'll make it work."

She relaxes in her seat, and I know my smile looks like a grimace.

"And what about you?" she presses.

I shake my head. "This is Danny's dream," I tell her. "Not mine."

COLTON

The deck is already pooled with water that's been driven beneath the open structure, and the trees circling the lodge are shaking in the wind. Branches and debris have been blown into the corridor.

I bow my head and start for the communal cabin. The smell of smoke from the fire is thick in the air, tangled with the storm.

When I walk in, Noah and Karly stop talking, but I notice Karly's face is blotchy from crying. She turns away from me and wipes quickly at her cheeks.

"Hey, Colton," Noah says. He sounds tired. He looks it, too, the way his eyes are sunken, and his movements seem heavy.

"Hey." I take a seat on the couch opposite.

The fire sounds loud, crackling in the hearth. The logs piled in the base are splintering, incinerating, and spitting embers onto the floorboards. Rain spatters through the chimney, encouraging the erratic movement of the flames.

Right after I sit down, Karly stands up. "Excuse me," she murmurs. She squeezes past the coffee table between us and heads for the front door.

"See you, Karly," Noah says.

"Be careful out there," I tell her, and she freezes, her fingers touching the door handle. There's a different kind of tension in her expression now, a knot of fear. "The storm's blown some branches into the corridor," I tell her. "Just watch out."

"Oh." She dips her gaze. "I know."

When the door clicks shut behind her, I bring my attention back to Noah.

He heaves a sigh and scrubs his hands through his hair. "We were just talking about that. Saying we should clear the corridor before it gets dark. I don't think we'll be leaving here anytime soon and the last thing we need is for someone to break an ankle tonight."

"Yeah. Good call." I pause for a second. "Hey, am I being paranoid, or did Karly only leave because I walked in?"

Noah locks his hands and stares down at the floorboards. "Yeah. You're not being paranoid."

I push the wet hair from my forehead. "Hit me with it, then. What, she thinks I killed Piper?"

He drags his hands over his face. Light stubble is building along his jaw, and his mouth is turned downward. "No," he says. "Not you."

"Danny?" I guess.

He doesn't answer. He doesn't need to. It's written all over his face.

"She thinks someone was with Piper when she fell," he says at last. "She says Eva heard a scream and someone running away, and now the girls all think Piper was *pushed*. And, yeah, she has some questions about Danny."

I clear my throat. "And you have the same questions, right?"

"I didn't say that."

I press my tongue hard to the roof of my mouth.

"Okay, listen," he says, meeting my eyes. "I know he's your brother, and you don't want to hear it, but maybe there's something in this. Danny found Piper, in some deep drop. He knew exactly where to look." He holds my stare and I rub the nape of my neck. "If he wrote some letter to Piper, and she turned him down—"

"They were just friends," I cut him off. "He didn't write the note."

"You believe that?" he asks.

"Yes."

"Okay."

There's a beat of silence between us, and his expression pulls into a grimace. "I hate this, Colton. I hate saying this. But Javier's been arrested, and, gut feeling—" he slaps his palm to his chest "—I don't think Javier did it. Do you?"

"No," I answer hoarsely.

"I'm worried about him, man. We've got to help him out."

"I know that. But Danny didn't do it, either."

"Then who?" he shoots back. "You? Me?"

The fire snaps and cracks between us.

"I don't know." I press my knuckles to my mouth. "Do the cops know something we don't? Javier and Piper were fighting yesterday."

Noah purses his lips. "Yeah," he says, nodding. "And it's possible, maybe, that things got out of hand…"

"He went looking for her last night," I take over, piecing the story together. "Found her at the cave. Told her it was over."

"Maybe she found out about Javier's plans for college, too," he says. "That he didn't really want to go with her, and she flipped. Then it got physical, and Piper lost her footing…"

"And Javier didn't know what to do, so he ran." I look down at the floor, and the timeworn scuffs on the wood.

"Could have happened that way," Noah finishes, tugging at the collar of his T-shirt. "Do you buy it?"

I don't have to think about my answer. "No."

"Me, either."

I lean forward. "Why would Piper have been alone in the cave in the middle of the night? Or with anyone in the cave? That's what I don't get."

He bites his thumb. "Unless she was meeting someone there, and they didn't want to be seen?" Immediately, I think of how I'd been planning to meet Eva out of sight so we could be alone. That was our plan.

The front door swings open, and we fall silent. Paul walks in, leaving wet footprints in the entry hall.

"Hi, boys." He shrugs out of his coat and hangs it on a hook on the back of the door, then he joins us on the couches, taking a seat beside Noah in the spot where Karly once was. "How are you doing?"

Noah summons a strained smile. "Trying to keep it together."

"Of course." Paul bows his head for a second. "I just got off the phone with your dad."

Noah swallows. "Yeah?"

"Roads have been closed with flooding, and there's been some landside south of Seattle. Your dad's looking into flights out later tonight as an alternative. He's going to keep me posted."

Noah cusses under his breath. "Not looking good, then."

"Let's just wait and see, eh?"

When they're together like this, I can see the family resemblance. They're both solidly built with shaggy blond hair and a strong jaw. Usually, I'd say they're both chilled out guys, but neither of them looks relaxed right now. They look broken.

They're probably thinking the same thing about me.

In the silence, Noah's words keep running through my mind. *Danny found Piper, in some deep drop. He knew exactly where to look.*

But he's my brother, and I trust him without question. I have to.

I turn my attention to the fire and watch the logs burn.

FIVE MONTHS EARLIER

I saw Noah go under. The nose of his board went up, and he went down.

I paddle against the current and help him get to the outcropping hanging over the water. I pull myself up onto the rocky ledge, then grip his hand and pull him up, too.

He sits on the ledge, hunched over with his hands braced on his knees. His face has turned almost green, and blond curls are stuck flat to his forehead. His shoulders are shaking, maybe from shock or from the cold November climate, and one side of his face is grazed and wet with blood and water.

"You alright?" I ask, clapping his back.

He nods, then he doubles over, coughing up water.

Javier must have seen because he's paddling toward us. A minute later, he's hauling his board, and himself, up onto the rock projection.

"What happened?" *he calls.*

Noah coughs again. With a groan, he leans back, locking his arms out straight behind him as he stares up at the gray sky. His left leg is cut up pretty bad, too. The rocks around here are savage.

Javier catches my attention and winces, and I shrug back.

We stay like this for a while, the three of us sitting on the outcropping. Behind us, the wind howls through an eroded rock cave.

"My folks are going to kill me," *Noah murmurs. He touches his face, checking for blood on his fingers.* "How bad is it?" *He looks at me, tilting his face for inspection.*

I squint back at him and the blood streaking his cheek. "You've looked better."

"And worse," *Javier jokes.*

"Shit," *Noah says under his breath.*

"You should probably go to the hospital," *I tell him.* "That might need stitches."

He touches the cut on his face and grimaces. "My dad's going to be so pissed," *he groans.* "I'm supposed to be going to his company function next week."

Javier laughs. "What do you care? You're not a suit like them." *He grins, a wide wicked smile.*

Noah manages a smile back, even with blood tracking toward his jaw. "I'm supposed to be making a good impression. They might want to hire me after college."

"Yeah?" Javier says, his teeth gleaming in the low light. "How about I go in your place? I wouldn't mind walking into a decent paycheck after college."

I laugh under my breath. "Yeah. That'd be nice."

Javier frowns at me. "I thought you weren't going to college."

My eyes stray away from him. "I'm not."

"What, you're changing your mind?" Noah asks, trying to catch my attention. When I don't respond, he adds, "It's not too late to send out applications. Over the summer, you seemed dead set on going."

"Yeah." Javier's heavy brows pull together. "Didn't you want to major in English?"

"I don't know," I brush them off. "I've got a good setup at Summits. That'll be better for me. I'd probably flunk out the first semester at college, anyway."

"True that," Javier says with a quick laugh. "Your brother got all the smart genes, huh?"

I force a smile. "Yeah."

Javier slaps my shoulder. "And he's got a hot girlfriend," he adds. "We should be taking notes."

Noah snorts. "You've got to be kidding me. I don't envy Danny dating Piper Meyers. You've seen what she posts about him. She burns him hard."

"Yeah, but…" Javier shrugs and grins. "Small price to pay. I'd trade places with Danny like that." He snaps his fingers.

"Whatever," I mutter. "I don't think they'll last much longer, anyway."

Javier's eyes stay on me. "Yeah? How come?"

"I don't know. Just a feeling." I stand and water drips from my board shorts. "Come on. You wanna go find Paul and see if we can get to a hospital?"

Noah groans as he hauls himself to his feet, and Javier follows his lead.

Drops of blood stain the rocks as we walk away.

Title: Audio File_Karly Davis Interview

Good morning. My name is Detective Brennan, and the time is ten-fifty a.m. on Saturday, April sixteenth. Can I take your name, please?

It's Karly Davis.

Hi, Karly. Why don't you go ahead and talk me through what happened here last night?

Okay. We had a fire on the beach, just talked and stuff. It was our last night. We were… We were just having fun.

The mood was good amongst your friends?

Yes. We were having a good time. We were happy, mostly.

Mostly? Who wasn't happy?

I guess maybe Javier and Danny.

I understand your friend Javier was at odds with his girlfriend, Piper. Is that correct?

Yes, that's right. They weren't speaking.

Do you know what they'd been arguing about?

Um, yes. Danny wrote a note to Piper, and it made Javier feel threatened. I'm not sure what was written in the note. Piper never actually saw it. At least, that's what she told me.

And how about your friend Danny? You say he didn't seem happy last night?

He didn't talk to us much, and he left the fire early.

Did he leave alone?

I didn't notice.

And Javier, did he leave the fire alone?

Yes. Well, he and Colton went to talk, and they were gone for a little while, so Piper went looking for them. When the boys came back without her, I told Javier she'd gone, and he went after her. But then he came back to the cabin and said he couldn't find her. He said he couldn't… I'm sorry. I'm finding this really hard.

Okay. Just take your time, Karly. Were you at the accommodations when Javier returned?

Yes. I talked to him. He seemed really stressed, and he said he thought Piper had been with Danny somewhere.

Did you see Danny back at the accommodations?

Yes. He was outside on the deck.

But Javier still thought Piper had been with Danny?

Yes. He was upset and paranoid, I think. Piper never would have cheated on him, if that's what he was thinking. She wasn't like that. She was really committed to him.

Karly, I need to ask you a tough question, okay? Do you believe that any of your friends might have harmed Piper Meyers?

(0:27 DELAY) I'm not answering any more questions.

PIPER

Okay, I'm literally about to leave for my trip. The girls will be here in… Oh, shit, literally any minute. Okay. So, I just wanted to let you all know that my DMs are always open if you ever need to talk. Senior year spring break was something I've dreamed about since I was a freshman. Honestly, I'd kind of imagined myself in Florida or Cabo, somewhere with a lot going on. Obviously, this trip to Oregon is going to be a little different. But Javier is really into surfing and all that fun stuff, so it'll be good. It's quality time with my people, anyway.

So, because it's such a big moment in our high school lives, we managed to convince our friend Miles Brynne to come with us. Miles is so adorable, he's all nerdy and little and I always just want to squish his cheeks, but he's been through a rough time lately. You've probably read about it online, and if you haven't, I suggest you google it. This shit is real. Pressure of school can get to anyone, so please, please, please, please check in with your friends. Let Miles's story be a caution to you all.

The short version is he got caught cheating, and he's facing the consequences of that. This is one of the many reasons why I'm so against cheating. It always comes out sooner or later. There's always someone who's going to talk. It's just not worth it, guys.

Okay, well, that's all I wanted to say. Stay true to you. Love you guys so, so much.

EVA

Karly's in the outer corridor with her hood pulled up to cover the damp and fluttering strands of her hair. She's untangling a large branch that's lodged between the railing posts and blocking the path.

She frowns at me as I climb the steps to the deck, taking in my wet hair and clothes.

"I've been talking to my parents." It's a weak explanation for why I'm soaked through and dripping with rainwater, but Karly looks too drained to care. It's partly true; I did call my parents. But I'm not ready to admit to Karly that before my phone call, I was out on the beach confronting Alice about the letter. I think that's Alice's story to tell.

Karly stands and brushes aside her bangs with the back of her hand. "Noah and Colton are in the communal room," she says. "I think they're going to come help clear the corridor, but I figured I'd get a head start." She offers me a weak smile. "I guess it's good to keep busy, you know?"

"Yeah," I murmur. I join her, setting to work moving the debris that's been swept in by the storm.

"I knocked on Alice and Miles's door, too," Karly adds, "but they were talking, and it seemed heavy. They said they'd be out in a minute." She exhales. "So I guess I'm on my own."

"I'm here now," I tell her. "You're not alone."

She nods.

The last few hours have thrown me for a loop. I've barely had time to process Alice being the person behind the note, let alone Danny's not-so-subtle suggestion that I get rid of Piper's phone.

But I know that getting rid of the phone isn't an option. Not if it contains any information that could make sense of what really happened to Piper. She needs justice, and we need the truth.

"My parents are worried," I relay to Karly as I dislodge a gnarled branch from the deck railings. "They said a lot of the roads coming into Tillamook have been closed, and flights out of Seattle are getting canceled. They're talking with Paul now, trying to figure out a plan."

"My mom just texted me, too," Karly whispers softly. "She said there are no more flights out of Seattle tonight."

My stomach rolls as I glance up at the grim sky. The rain is getting heavier, and beyond the cabins, the waves are even wilder, rising high and exploding against the shore.

My phone pings in my coat pocket, and I slip it free.

Mom: Two major roads officially closed. Hang in there, honey.

The storm should pass tonight, and we'll be there first thing to-morrow.

Dad: We've contacted the local police and they're having clo-sures on their end, too. They've suggested you stay put. Stay at the cabins with Paul. We'll be there first thing.

"Travel out of Seattle isn't happening tonight," I tell Karly. She stops and takes a small breath.

"Karly," I say, catching her gaze. "You know I didn't do it, right? I didn't push Piper." My heart beats a little faster while I wait for her response.

"I know," she answers quietly. "For a second, I wondered…" I press my lips together.

"Because of the phone," she adds. "You had her phone, Eva. You must have gotten pretty close to her."

I think of Piper's phone, still hidden in my room. A piece of Piper still lingering.

My throat feels tight when I answer. "I *was* close to her," I say, swallowing. "I just didn't realize it at the time. If I'd have just looked around the cave a little more, maybe I could have…" A ragged breath escapes me. "Maybe I could have helped her."

Karly's gaze dips. "Don't do that to yourself. It was dark, you couldn't have seen her." Then, faintly, she adds, "It wasn't me, either. In case it ever crossed your mind."

"I know," I murmur.

"And Javier," she says in a hoarse voice. "I just don't be-lieve it." Her eyes land on mine, and she bites her lip. "Do you think he's okay?"

"I hope so. Maybe we could call the station if he isn't back soon, check up on him?"

"Yeah." She pauses and her gaze strays to the surrounding forest. "Who did this, Eva?" Her stare lands on me as she waits for an answer.

I can see it in her eyes. That searching look. She has a name, and she wants to say it, her lips almost ready to move.

But I know whose name she's going to say, and I don't want to hear it. Instead, I turn my attention to the cove. Specifically, the cave in the distance. The tide has risen and is already starting to flood the entrance. Before I have time to think about it, I'm heading for the steps.

"Eva," Karly calls after me. She lets the branch drop to the planked floor. "Look, I'm not accusing anyone. I'm sorry, I just—"

I stop and turn to her. "It's not that. There's something I need to do."

She frowns. "What?"

"I have to go back to the cave," I tell her, zipping my jacket and flipping the hood.

Her lips part. "What? Right now?" Her eyes wander skyward to the rain that's lashing beyond the shelter.

"The tide hasn't come in yet, and if I don't do this now, who knows if I'll get another chance." I glance farther along the corridor and lower my voice. "Karly, I heard Piper scream last night. Whoever was with her ran away. But they weren't running back to the lodge, they were heading in the opposite direction." Her eyes are locked on mine, listening intently as I muddle through my thoughts. So I keep going. "When I got to the lodge a few minutes later, Danny was there. I need to go to the cave and retrace my steps to see if he could have doubled back and gotten past me without me noticing." Her eyes wander along the corridor to the room that Colton and Danny share.

"You can't go out alone in this weather," she says in a thin voice. "It could be dangerous. After what happened to Piper…"

"I'll be okay."

But she's already heading for the steps after me.

"What?" she asks, quirking an eyebrow at my expression. "I'm coming with you. If you can be reckless, I can be, too."

I muster a smile. "We can be reckless together. Maybe we'll cancel each other out."

"Let's hope," she says with a jittery laugh.

We brace against the wind as we leave the shelter of the corridor, heading into the rain and down the slippery stone steps toward the sand. The grains aren't soft and fine like they were yesterday. Now, the sand feels like thick sludge, and we sink deeper into it with every step. The gale whips at our coats as we forge a path toward the mouth of the cave.

An icy chill moves over me—not from the cold wind or jarring rain. I was *here*, just last night, standing in the darkness with my phone's flashlight carving a path to the rocks.

The police have marked off the entrance to the cave with a single stretch of yellow tape that's tremoring and snapping in the gale.

"I heard the stones click," I tell Karly, pointing to the pebbled route leading away from the cave.

"Okay," she says, shielding her eyes from the storm.

"So whoever ran must have been right here."

With Karly following close behind, I climb over the rocks,

and small stones clack with our every stride. If someone had been heading to the lodge from here, I would have heard their footsteps, the click of stones and pebbles underfoot.

"I was probably in the cave for less than a minute," I explain to Karly, raising my voice to be heard above the storm. "It was a calm and still night. Surely, I would have heard Danny, or whoever, pass me to get back to the lodge. But I didn't. Whoever it was went the other way."

Karly's gaze lands on the cave, and she swallows. The wind tosses around the loose strands of her hair. "So, you don't think it was Danny?" she asks, wrapping her arms around herself.

I shake my head. "I don't see how it could have been. I'm sure I would have seen him or heard him. When I got to the lodge right after, he wasn't out of breath or rattled at all. It looked like he'd been there for a while."

Her shoulders shake as a shudder moves over her. "Okay," she murmurs. "If you're sure…"

"I am," I say. "Danny didn't do it. I know he didn't."

"But he was alone," Karly says.

The wind howls and I shiver. "I know," I answer. "But he wasn't the only one."

Title: Audio File_Miles Brynne Interview

My name is Detective Brennan, and it is eleven-fifteen in the morning, Saturday, April sixteenth. Can I take your name, please?

Certainly, of course. It's Miles Brynne.

Thank you, Miles. Why don't you go ahead and talk me through your account of what happened here last night?

Absolutely. We were on the beach, all nine of us. Everyone seemed to be in high spirits. I was talking to my friend Danny mostly. We haven't seen each other in a while, and it was good to catch up.

You haven't seen each other in a while? You don't attend the same school?

No. I mean, I did. I've been off school, and I haven't seen my friends for a few weeks.

Right.

Yes. Yes, it's been nice to see everyone.

Okay. Going back to last night, at what point did you return to the accommodations?

It was seven minutes past midnight.

That's very accurate.

I remember checking my watch when we got back.

We?

I was with my friend Alice.

Were you with Alice when you left the group on the beach?

Yes.

Were you alone at any point in the evening, Miles?

No. I was with the others on the beach, and then Alice during the walk back. Alice and I have been sharing a room, too. We were together the whole time. Yes, I'm absolutely certain of that.

In your opinion, did any of your friends have reason to harm Piper Meyers?

No. Everyone loves Piper. *Loved*, I mean.

EVA

When we get back to the lodge, Noah and Colton are at either end of the corridor, clearing the path. Karly lowers her gaze and retreats to our room without a word, soaked through and shivering.

I see Noah's eyebrows pull together as he looks between me and the closed door where Karly disappeared, but I just summon a smile in response.

"Hey," I murmur to Colton as I approach him. "Where's Danny?"

"He's in our room, I think." Colton frowns. "Why? Is everything okay?"

I nod. "Can we talk?"

"Sure," he says, his brow creasing.

I start for Colton and Danny's room, and he follows me.

Inside, Danny is standing on his bed, working a screwdriver into a loose plank in the ceiling. A cooking pot is placed beneath the leaking roof, catching the steady drips. When we step into the room and the door falls shut behind us, Danny turns to stare at us silently, as we stand there, windswept and dripping rainwater onto the floorboards.

I draw in a breath. "Danny didn't do it," I announce. "What happened to Piper, I mean. Danny didn't do it."

He rolls his eyes as he jumps down from the bed.

"I already know *I* didn't do it," he says. "But thanks for sharing."

"Wait, what do you mean?" Colton takes a seat on his bed and leans forward, clasping his hands together. "How are you so sure?"

Danny shoots him a withering look.

"I was at the cave when Piper fell and I heard the stones stir when someone ran away," I explain quickly. "No footsteps passed me. I used my phone's flashlight around the cave and then the whole way back to the lodge where I found Danny on the deck. It would have been near impossible for Danny to pass me without me noticing, unless he'd run at full speed, but then he would have been out of breath by the time I saw him."

Danny rolls his eyes again. "*Near* impossible, but not totally. Thanks, Eva."

"Anyway," I say, waving my hand, "the point is, Danny wasn't the person in the cave with Piper last night." I press my hands to my heart. "I know it."

Colton smiles. Then he turns his smile toward Danny, who frowns back at him.

"It's not that I didn't trust you, Danny," I tell him, gently.

"I just wanted proof, for *you*. One of us did this, and you…" A little hesitantly, I meet his eyes. "You found her."

"Yeah," he says, running a hand over his mouth. "And I have to live with that memory. You guys aren't asking me how I feel, you're just treating me like a suspect."

I swap a glance with Colton.

"Maybe I should start treating you two like suspects," Danny says, gesturing between us with the screwdriver. "How do I know that you aren't lying?"

The gesture makes me flinch, and Colton heaves a sigh.

"Unlike you guys," Danny grits out, "I liked Piper. She was my friend and I cared about her."

Colton stares down at his hands.

"Danny," I murmur. "I'm sorry. I liked Piper, too."

"Yeah, okay, maybe *you* did," he says to me. Then his gaze slides to Colton. "But you didn't."

There's a breath of silence. Colton doesn't disagree with the comment. Because what would be the point? We all felt the tension between him and Piper; it was no secret.

"Let's not turn against each other," I implore, pressing my palms together. "We're on the same side."

"It doesn't feel like it," Danny mutters.

Colton stares at him from across the room. "There's something, though, isn't there? Something you're not saying."

Danny's eyebrows knit. "No." But a flush begins to creep into his neck. "What are you talking about?"

Colton's focus stays on him for a moment longer. "I don't know."

"Okay." Danny slaps his hands together and stands. "Well, now that we've got that out of the way, can I carry on with this?" He gestures to the loose ceiling plank with the screw-driver.

While Danny climbs onto the bed and starts working the bolt, my eyes land on Colton. The muscles in his jaw tighten.

"Did you guys manage to get hold of your mom?" I ask.

"Not yet," Colton says, and Danny makes a sound through his teeth. He starts working the screwdriver a little more forcefully. Across the room, rainwater drips from another leak, spattering the floorboards.

"I spoke to my parents," I tell them. "But it doesn't look like anyone will be traveling out tonight because of the storm."

Colton holds my stare and says nothing.

"We've just got to get through tonight," I add. "Then we can make sense of everything in the morning. Maybe the police will let us talk to Javier."

"I was thinking I should call the station," Colton says, his gaze flickering to Danny. "Explain to them that I was wrong, and that I was with Javier at the time—"

"What?" Danny's face falls. "And where does that leave me?"

"We'll figure it out. I'll say I was with Javier, then went back to the lodge to meet you—"

"You can't have been with both of us," Danny cuts him off, and his eyes narrow. "You were either with me or him."

Colton starts to speak, but the conversation is cut short when a frantic shout comes from the corridor.

EVA

I fling open the door to the corridor. Colton and Danny are off their beds fast and right behind me.

Farther along the deck, Alice gestures to us from outside Miles's room, where the door is ajar. "I need help," she shouts, waving us over.

As Colton, Danny, and I race along the corridor toward Alice, more doors swing open. Karly from our room, and Noah from the next along.

"Miles isn't doing so good," Alice explains.

She pushes the door wider, and suddenly I'm looking at Miles. He's doubled over on his bed, and he's shaking. His fingers are knotted through his pale hair, turned white by his grasp.

Alice catches my gaze. "We had a huge fight," she whispers, hugging her arms around herself.

"Oh, great," Miles says with a sharp breath when he sees

us crowded in the doorway. Alice, Colton, Danny, and me with Karly and Noah standing anxiously behind us. His hands tremble as he rakes them through his hair. "An audience."

"Miles." I move toward him, but he lifts his palm.

"Please," he says, stopping me in my tracks. "I just need some space." He folds into himself on the bed.

I glance at Danny, and he shakes his head in response.

"Miles," I broach carefully. "Are you okay?"

His mouth tightens. "Do I look okay, Eva?"

I glance at Danny again, waiting for him to step in. But he's gnawing on his lip now, concern furrowing his brow. He's not speaking.

"You can talk to us," I urge Miles. "We're all here for you. We're in this together."

He chokes out a bitter laugh. "Funnily enough, I don't feel like talking right now," he says. "I shouldn't even be here. I *wouldn't* be here if it weren't for you."

Me. His curt remark was directed at me.

It takes me aback to hear his voice so clipped, so angry. Miles. *Miles*, who prides himself on being too logical to ever lose his cool, is mad at me. For the first time in our entire friendship, he's genuinely mad at me. Because *I'm* the one who convinced him to come on this trip. Because *I* thought it'd be good for him. Or maybe I thought it'd be good for me. Because, honestly, it's been a while and I've missed him.

"Come on, Miles," Colton mutters. "Don't take it out on Eva. She's just trying to help."

Miles gives way to another strange laugh. "Oh, are you?" His stare is fixed on me, eyes narrowed. "Forgive me for being paranoid, but I'm finding it a little hard to trust anyone right now."

With that, my heart feels like it's dropped through the floorboards. He isn't talking about Piper.

"The police officer was questioning me about school," he says, tapping his knuckles together. He's staring at his hands, refusing to look at any of us. "And I just… I keep going over it in my mind, trying to make the pieces fit. The detective. When she interviewed me, she asked why I haven't been in school lately. And then it occurred to me, she must know about what happened."

My eyes wander over the group gathered in the doorway. A damp wind funnels through the open space, fluttering the curtains.

Rigid on his bed, Miles looks pale, sick, and his thin shoulders are shaking. "My situation at school has nothing to do with Piper," he says, jutting out his chin. "Or does it? Why were they asking?" His eyes are back on me now. Only me.

All I can do is shake my head. "You're reading too much into this," I manage.

"Am I?" he murmurs. His cold stare moves over the others, one at a time. "If Piper was the anonymous tip-off to the school about me, then the police might think I killed her because of it."

It feels as though the room has suddenly dropped a couple of degrees.

"So, was it her?" he presses. "Was it Piper who told the school I'd been selling test papers? Or was it one of you? Let's get to the bottom of this right now."

My pulse quickens. Here it is. The off-limits topic that the rest of us had agreed not to talk about, not to pressure *Miles* into talking about. Finally, after weeks of silence, he's talking.

COLTON

"What's going on out here?" Paul's voice makes us all turn. He's standing in the corridor, his brow lined beneath his disheveled blond hair. "Everyone okay?" He looks past us into the room where Miles is hunched on the bed.

"Everything's fine," Miles calls back tightly, and Paul frowns.

"Okay," he says slowly.

Miles's head stays bowed. "Could you all just leave me alone? Please."

Eva shoots me a helpless look.

"If none of you are willing to talk," Miles mutters, "then I'm not willing to, either."

"We don't have the answers you're looking for," Eva says softly.

Miles exhales. "Just… I need some time to myself."

Eva glances at me again, so I reach for her hand. "Come

on," I murmur, threading my fingers through hers. "Let's give him some space."

While everyone else disbands, whispering between one another, and Paul looks to Noah for some clarity, Eva and I begin moving along the corridor. We don't speak about where we're going—we just go.

We pass our rooms and continue along the deck, skirting around the side of the building and then down the stone steps onto the beach. Rain is falling heavily, but I don't care, and I don't think she does, either.

Whatever's left of the dull day is about to disappear. The light is slowly dimming. We lean close to the rock wall, taking some shelter. Eva sinks into me, falling into a hug, and I draw her closer as I stare out at the wild tide.

I find my voice. "I'm sorry."

She takes a deep breath. "It's not your fault, Colton." Then she moves back from me, but her hand stays on my arm and her fingers coil around my sleeve. "Do you think Miles is right? Do you think Piper was the person who tipped off the school about him?"

"Maybe." I stare out at the horizon. It's darkened by shadows and storm clouds.

"Piper used to talk about it a lot," Eva says, "in her videos. About Miles's situation."

I turn to her and frown. "So, what, Piper was taunting him?"

She sighs into the wind. "I used to think it was an accident, that Piper just wasn't aware of Miles's feelings. But now, I'm wondering..." The sentence falls away.

I drag my hand over my brow. "Yeah. I'm wondering the same thing."

She looks up to meet my eyes. Her grip tightens on my arm when she says the words. "In that final video, Piper said, *I'm going to tell everyone what you did.*"

I glance toward the lodge. "Okay, but if this *was* about Miles, she'd already done that. If Piper was the person who tipped off the school, the secret is already out. There's no one left to tell."

"But…" She hesitates and bites her lip. "Miles says he didn't do it. He says it wasn't him selling test papers."

I keep my eyes on hers. "What are you thinking?"

The wind whips a strand of hair across her cheekbone. "Maybe Piper had proof?" she says, her voice wavering. "Or maybe it *wasn't* Miles who'd been selling the papers, and she had proof of that." She squeezes her eyes shut for a second. "We need to talk to Miles. We need to know the whole story from his side."

"I agree," I tell her with a nod. "Let's give him a minute, though. He'll come around."

"I hope so," she whispers. "I hate that he's mad at me. I hate all of this."

I lock my arm around her. "I do, too," I murmur.

She leans into me, and I hold her closer, wondering if she can feel how fast my heart is beating.

PIPER

Hey, loves! So, we are on day two of our trip and having the best time.

As you can see, I'm still in bed and I know I look like such a hot mess right now. I've literally just woken up, not even kidding. I know, I know, it's practically the afternoon. Don't judge me!

Okay, I'm going to try to show you the boys from the window. Hold on. Okay, they're all out on the beach. A couple of them have their surfboards. That's Danny right there... Oh, wait. No. That's Colton, Danny's brother. Not my favorite person, guys, if I'm being totally honest. But that's life. You can't vibe with everyone, and our energies just do not match.

Zooming in farther along the beach. Miles is there, too, so that's nice. Isn't he just the cutest in his colorful clothes? Poor

Milesy-boo, he's been through a stressful time recently, and, as many of you probably know, he's been accused of doing some things that I'm sure he's not proud of. It must be wild for him to think that someone talked, but he might never find out who. That would sketch me out so bad, guys.

Anyway, I won't go into detail. Because it's okay to keep some things private. Everyone has secrets, right? Guys, even me, believe it or not! I have secrets that would make a lot of people very uncomfortable!

But that's a whole other video. I'll tell you about them one day when the time is right, promise.

Title: Audio File_Noah Lauder Interview

Good morning. The time is approximately ten-thirty a.m. on Saturday, April sixteenth. My name is Detective Brennan. Can you state your full name for the purpose of the recording, please?

Noah William Lauder.

Noah, how would you describe the relationship between your friends Piper Meyers and Javier Ramos?

Uh, yeah. They've been dating for a couple of months, and they were really into each other. Javier…he had strong feelings. I know he did. They both did.

Some of your friends have said that Piper and Javier were arguing last night. I'd really appreciate your honesty here, Noah. I'd like to remind you how serious this is.

No, I get that. I mean, I think Javier was only mad because he thought Danny was interested in Piper, his girlfriend, right? Danny wrote her a note or something. But I didn't talk to Javier about it. I don't get involved in that stuff. Colton talked to him last night, though. You should ask him.

Does Javier have a history of violence?

No. Not at all. That thing with Danny was a one-off. Whatever you've been told, it was out of character for Javier to react that way.

What thing is this?

Uh. It was nothing. Just, they got into an argument, about the note. But it wasn't anything.

I see. In your opinion, did any of your friends have reason to harm Piper Meyers?

(0:10 DELAY) No. No, of course not.

I'm going to ask you that question again, Noah. Did any of your friends have reason to harm Piper Meyers?

Not my friends.

EVA

I follow Colton back to the lodge. Somewhere along the way, his hand folded around mine, and now I don't want to let go. It's a comfort I didn't know I needed until right now. As darkness creeps up on us, and the storm shakes the trees, I don't want to let go.

Danny's in their room, slouched on his bed, shoulders curled forward. He looks up when we walk through the door and frowns at our wet hair and clothes. His gaze travels to our joined hands, and his eyebrows raise.

"Is everything okay?" he asks slowly.

I nod, struggling for an answer. What constitutes *okay* right now?

But Danny doesn't press.

Colton closes the door behind us, and we leave wet foot-prints as we make our way to his side. Taking a seat on his bed, I start combing my fingers through my hair, shivering as the cold sets in. Rain taps on the windowpanes, and constant rivulets streak the glass.

"Dunno what got into Miles," Danny says. "Don't take it personally, Eva. It's just everything, and this place…"

"I know," I say. Then I meet his eyes. "I've been thinking a lot about what you said, Danny." My voice sounds weak. "About Piper's phone." Colton moves his thumb along mine—that gentle reminder that he's here. It catches me off guard for a second, how natural this feels, how calming. I let that feeling envelop me as I say the words, "I'm going to hand Piper's phone over to the police. I should have done it hours ago, whatever the consequences."

Danny rubs his brow with the heels of his hands. "Eva…"

"I get it, Danny," I say. "It won't look good. But the police need this evidence. Piper was murdered."

"You don't know that for sure," he says, leaning forward and locking his hands. "Anyway, what difference will it make if you hand the phone in now? Other than making you seem guilty?"

"It's not just a phone, though, is it?" I shoot back. "The video could be vital evidence. *We* might not be able to see who was with Piper in the cave, but the police, and their access to advanced technology…" I trail off when I notice his face change. His brow creases.

"Video?" he says, blinking at me. "What video?"

I glance between him and Colton. "The video on Piper's phone. The one that she took right before she fell." I look at Colton and frown. "I thought you said you told him?"

Colton's eyes stray to Danny, then come back to me. "All I

said was that you'd found Piper's phone in the cave after you heard her scream. And that we saw a picture of the note on it."

Danny's knee starts bouncing. "This is huge," he says. He presses his knuckles to his mouth. "What was on the video?"

I shake my head. "It was too dark to see anything, but Piper was with someone, talking to them. She was angry. She told them to stop threatening her, and she said she was going to tell everyone what they'd done. Then she screamed, and it ended."

Danny's Adam's apple bobs. "Can I see it?"

"Yeah, I guess. It's in my room. I'll get it." Reluctantly, I let my hand slip from Colton's. He looks up at me as I stand and begin for the door. Leaving them alone, I retreat into the dim evening and head for my own room.

Karly isn't in there, but her luggage is propped against the bed frame, just waiting to leave. My cell is on the pine nightstand, and I quickly plug it into the charger before its battery dies completely. It takes me a second to notice that Piper's phone, which had been charging on the nightstand, too, isn't there anymore.

I check around my side, moving bedding, rummaging through my bag, the furniture, then Karly's bedding.

But Piper's phone isn't anywhere.

I leave the room and pace fast along the corridor. I know Miles asked for space, but I've got to find Alice, or Karly, to see if either of them have the phone, or if they moved it while I was gone.

Coming to a stop outside Miles's door, I straighten my shoulders and tap on the wood.

"Alice?" I call. "Are you in there?"

After a moment, when no one responds, I twist the handle and push the door ajar.

There's no one there.

Something seems different about the room, though. I was just here, an hour ago or less, but now…

My breath falters as the realization dawns on me.

Alice's luggage is at the foot of her bed, and her sweater is draped over the wicker chair, but I can't see any of Miles's belongings, nothing.

And his backpack is gone.

DMEA GROUP CHAT

EVA: Miles, where are you? Please check in.

ALICE: We're so worried, Miles. Please call us or text us, anything to let us know you're okay.

DANNY: You're not on your own in this. If you come back, we'll talk.

ALICE: Come on, Miles.

EVA: I've told Paul you're gone. I'm sorry, Miles. Don't hate me.

ALICE: Please be safe, wherever you are.

COLTON

There are six of us now. Six of us left.

We're all in the communal room, Alice, Karly, and Noah on one couch and Eva, Danny, and me on the other. The fire is burning low, and once again Paul is standing in the kitchen with his cell pressed to his ear. He's been trying to call Miles's number every couple of minutes for the past two hours. It keeps going to voice mail.

I look across the coffee table at Noah. He's biting his thumb, tapping his nail against his teeth. It's like the six of us are playing a game of chicken, no one daring to be the first to leave. No one daring to talk, either. But we're wired, on edge. I feel it.

The wind is howling outside, shaking the windows. The storm's getting worse, and we're all trapped.

Karly fiddles with a strand of her hair. "Where do you

think he went?" Her voice breaks the strange silence that had formed between us.

Alice's gaze strays to the front door. "I don't know. But he shouldn't be out there alone."

The fire flickers weakly, and the mounted antlers throw long clawed shadows over the room. Paul ends his call and strides into the living room. His car keys are in his fist.

"Right," he says with a tense breath, "still no luck getting through to Miles's cell. I'm going to go out in the car, see if I can find him."

Noah's already shaking his head. "I don't think you should do that. The roads are bad, and it's dark out now…"

Paul rubs his jaw. "All the more reason to find Miles quickly," he says. "The rest of you—" he aims his car key at us "—do not leave this lodge. Okay? I'll be back soon, hopefully with Miles."

We muster a few weak responses as he heads for the door. A moment later, we hear his car engine rumble.

Eva gives way to a small breath. "Miles must have been so scared if he thought his only option was to run. What possessed him to just leave like this, without telling any of us?"

"Maybe he did it." The words escape before I have a chance to think them through. Next to me, Eva tenses. She looks at me.

"What do you mean?" she asks.

I tap on the arm of the couch. "Maybe Miles killed Piper."

Everyone is pin-drop silent and staring at me.

"Miles?" Eva blinks like she can't believe those words just came from me.

I clear my throat. "Because he said it, didn't he? He thought

Piper was the person who told the school about him selling test papers."

Eva chokes out a sound, and my lungs tighten. Up until now, we've been on the same side, together. But now she's looking at me like I've betrayed her, and it doesn't feel good.

"He wasn't selling papers," she says firmly. "He was framed for it."

"Do you really believe that?" Noah asks from across the table. His eyes are on Eva, and he's waiting for a response. I figure he's trying to back me up, but it isn't helping. Her face falls, and he just keeps talking. "They tracked Miles through the computer system," Noah says. "They had the footprint from when he logged on and when the tests were downloaded, that's what I heard."

"They could have gotten it wrong." Danny's voice is cold.

From across the table, Karly's gaze lingers on him. "That would be unlikely, though, wouldn't it?"

Danny falls silent, and my shoulders tighten. No good can come of this debate, especially with three of Miles's closest friends in the room. None of them are going to want to hear this. "Look," I jump in, "all I meant was, Miles had motive. *Might* have had motive."

"*You* had motive, Colton," Karly says, her eyes landing on me now. "Piper said you hated her, and we all saw it." She pauses, glances at Danny, then adds, "Just saying."

Danny sits taller. "Alright. If we're going to do this, then let's go." He slaps his hands together. "We'll go around the room and say who we each think did it."

I squeeze my eyes shut. Next to me, Eva sighs.

"Who is this helping?" she asks sharply.

"I want to know," Danny says. "Don't you? Don't you want to know if any of your friends think you're a murderer?"

"No."

"I'll go first," Danny pushes on. There's a bite to his voice, a venom that I don't hear on him often. "I think it was Javier." Just like that, no pause, no remorse for saying it. Just done.

He looks at Alice on the couch opposite. "Al," he says, gesturing for her to speak. "Your turn."

She hesitates, and for a second, I think she's going to refuse to answer. And I realize I'm hoping she does refuse, because Eva's right, who is this helping? But then Alice speaks, so softly I can barely hear her. "I don't know." Then after a pause, "But if it was Miles—"

Eva sucks in a breath. "Alice, how can you say that?"

She lowers her gaze. "I'm sorry," she says. "But I don't know. I just... Miles has been acting so strangely, Eva. I've been rooming with him, remember? I've seen him twitching, talking to himself, snapping over the smallest stuff. We got into an argument right before he had that panic attack." Her gaze travels over us. "I told him I thought we should tell the police that..." She stops short.

"What?" Karly presses.

She takes a breath. "That we weren't together the *entire* time last night," she finishes quietly. "Miles didn't want to change his statement. And now he's gone."

"That doesn't mean anything," Eva jumps in quickly. "He might have just needed some time to think, to clear his head."

Alice's gaze strays to the dark window. "I get that. But the police told us to stay here. This storm is no joke, and Miles just walked right out into it."

"Because he's scared," Eva says, though her voice doesn't carry as much conviction this time.

"I'm not saying that I think Miles…" Alice trails off and swallows. "Maybe it was an accident."

"It wasn't Miles," Danny mutters.

Karly tilts her head. "Well, I actually don't think it was Miles, either. I think it was Colton or Danny." She doesn't break eye contact when she says my name.

My heart starts hammering in my chest. I don't move. No one does. We're all frozen, like coiled springs.

"Wait." Alice holds up her hands. "Is this about the note?" She looks at Karly in the seat beside her. "Please don't be suspicious of Danny because of the note. He didn't write it, I did."

Now everyone's attention is back on her, and my mind is racing.

"Just…" She lets out a fractured breath. "Don't blame Danny, it was all me. If you're going to doubt anyone over the note, then doubt me."

Karly's gaze drifts to the floor. "Okay. But that's not why I said Danny's name."

"Okay. Well, good." Alice raises her chin. I see her catch Danny's eye, and she nods. He mirrors the gesture.

Noah clears his throat. "Alright, well, I'm saying Miles," he mumbles, but I see his eyes go to Danny. I didn't miss that inadvertent glance; I doubt anyone did. I'm just glad he didn't speak his true feelings out loud.

And then it's on me. They're all looking at me, waiting.

"You all know what I think," I say. "I don't need to say it again."

Eva folds her arms, her elbow bumping against mine. "And

don't include me in this witch hunt," she snaps. "Frankly, I don't think any of us are capable, otherwise I wouldn't be on this trip. And while we're in here speculating on Miles's innocence, he could be in serious danger out there alone." She gestures to the pitch-black night beyond the rained-streaked windowpanes.

"Yeah," Danny says. "Maybe whoever killed Piper has gone after Miles, too. Because maybe Miles figured it out, and they wanted to keep him quiet."

Karly sucks in a breath.

Next to me, Eva stands abruptly. "This is ridiculous," she says. She sidles past me and starts toward the door.

"Where are you going?" I call.

"To look for Miles." She swings the front door open, letting in a rush of cold air.

I'm on my feet now, too, and I follow, because I don't know what else to do. The others are calling after us, but we're not turning back. Suddenly, I'm outside in the darkness, shielding my eyes from the storm, stumbling down the wooden porch steps, and sinking into mud as I walk blindly into the night. I can't see her. I can't hear anything above the forest groaning in the gale.

"Eva!" I shout, but my voice is stolen by the wind.

Title: Audio File_Paul Lauder Interview

Recording commenced at approximately twelve p.m. on Saturday, April sixteenth. Good afternoon, my name is Detective Brennan. Can you confirm your full name, please?

Paul Lauder. I'm the owner of the property.

Mr. Lauder, thank you for arriving so quickly this morning. Could you give me some more information on the arrangement this group of minors has with you at the property?

They're a good bunch of kids, trustworthy. My nephew Noah and his buddies. I let them use the place for a couple of days over their spring break. They're good kids.

I assume you're familiar with the group, your nephew's friends?

Yes, I've met a couple of the boys before. The brothers, Colton and Danny, and Noah's friend Javier, they all came to stay with me for a weekend last winter right after I first bought this place.

Had you previously met the victim, Piper Meyers?

No. I mean, I'd heard her name mentioned by the boys. They all thought very highly of her. Detective Brennan, I am beyond devastated that this has happened. I assume the family has been notified?

Yes, they have been informed and I can confirm that they are being supported through these difficult circumstances.

Right. Please, if there's anything I can do, to reach out to them and express my sincere condolences.

I'll be sure to let you know. Mr. Lauder, you said you'd heard the boys talking about Ms. Meyers. Can you elaborate on that at all?

(0:09 DELAY) Only that the boys mentioned her name. I remember they showed me a social media video on their phones, one of Piper's. She seemed like such a bright and charismatic girl. It's devastating. I keep thinking, maybe if I'd been here to supervise… But Noah's eighteen years old. Most of them are. And I've been close by in the area in case they needed anything.

Mr. Lauder, are you aware of any reason why an altercation might have taken place here last night?

No. Absolutely not. The caves around here are extremely dangerous, Detective Brennan. Rest assured, I'll be placing hazard signs at the rocks ahead of opening the grounds to the public. An accident like this will not happen again, I can assure you of that.

EVA

I feel Colton's hand reach for mine in the darkness.

"What are you doing?" he half yells. The night is disorienting, muddling. I know the lodge is behind us; I can see the glow of the fire coming from inside the cabin, but everything ahead is lost in an abyss. I don't know where the forest begins or what I'm even walking toward.

"I have to find Miles." I sound breathless. Too loud, too frantic. "What if Danny's right? What if whoever killed Piper has done something to Miles, too? Maybe whatever it was that Piper knew, Miles knew, too." I slip my hand free from Colton's. "We have to find him."

"Eva, this is a bad idea," he says in a ragged voice. "Please. Please don't go out in this. You have no idea where Miles might have gone." He reaches for my hand again, and I let his fingers fold around mine, a touch of warmth in the cold air. "We'll call the police. We'll get a search party out looking for him or something."

I swallow down a painful lump in my throat. "But imagine how that's going to look? If we tell the police Miles has left the lodge, then they'll think he had something to do with what happened to Piper and he's trying to run. Even Alice thinks that and she's his friend."

"Okay," Colton says calmly, his hand still sealed around mine. "Then we'll come up with a better idea. Just not this."

"Piper's phone is missing," I blurt out. "I think someone's taken it."

There's a beat of silence, and it feels like an eternity before Colton speaks again.

"Okay," he says at last. "We'll figure it out. Just don't leave."

I can't answer. I can't find the words. But I let him lead me through the darkness, back toward the blinking porch light. We feel our way up the steps and into the shelter of his room.

The bulb glows weakly, illuminating the pine walls and tired furniture. It highlights the shadows, too.

I take a seat on the bed as Colton crosses the room and crouches at his backpack. A moment later, he hands me a towel.

"Thanks," I murmur, wrapping it around my shoulders and shivering as rainwater crawls down my face.

Colton sits beside me on the bed. "Miles will be okay," he says. His gaze is fixed on the opposite wall, broad shoulders hunched forward. "Don't listen to Danny. It's just *his* paranoia. Don't let it get to you."

I study Colton's profile—he's calm, breathing steadily. He always gives off this air of someone so stable, so in control no matter how hard his life is thrown off-kilter. "How can you be so sure?" I whisper.

He turns to me and musters a smile, the faintest dimple appearing in his cheek. "Because someone has to be."

I summon a smile back. "Yeah, I guess so." In this quiet moment between us, I gaze into his eyes. "I don't know how you always manage to keep it together. It's quite the skill you have there."

He grins and looks down at his hands. "Yeah, not really. It's all an act. Trust me, inside, I'm losing it worse than anyone."

I laugh quietly. "You cover it well."

His eyes return to me. "Eva, I lied to you the other day."

The words make me stop. For a second, I can't find my voice. "About what?" I ask weakly.

He musses his hair. "I *did* want to go to college. I was going to go, that was the plan. Did Danny tell you?"

I shake my head, keeping my focus on him.

"We had the money and everything," he says. "My grandparents' savings. They were going to pay for us to go."

"They changed their mind?" I venture.

"No." He starts gnawing on his lower lip. "We were all set. They transferred the money into my mom's account and all that. I knew where I was applying, we were good to go. *But*," he draws out the word, "then my mom lost her job and she thought if she gambled the money on a sure thing, she'd make it back and then some."

"It wasn't a sure thing," I murmur.

"Yeah." He presses his lips together. "She lost. And we all lost."

"Oh, no," I breathe, touching my hand to my heart. "Colton, I'm so sorry."

"It's okay." He forces a smile. But I can tell from the stricken look on his face that this is anything but okay.

"Danny's still going, though…"

"Yeah," he says. "Danny's been saving, we both have. He should be the one to go. He's got more potential than I have."

Those words make my heart ache for him, because I know he truly believes them. "That's not true," I say, touching his hand.

"Anyway," he keeps going, staring distantly at the shadowed wall opposite us, "right before we left for the trip, my mom came home late. She'd been out with some friends, and we saw a receipt from the casino they'd been at. She'd dropped some serious cash that night. And Danny…" He pauses and shakes his head at the memory. "Danny lost it with her. He didn't hold back. Then I got involved, too, and things got bad between the three of us. Things got said."

"I can imagine."

"But it didn't feel good," he mutters. "It's not her fault, you know? She's got a problem and she needs… She needs help. She needs us."

I take a slow breath. "Do your grandparents know about what happened to the money?"

He locks his hands and bows his head. "No. We're going to act like I'm still going."

My eyebrows shoot up. "You're going to keep that up for four years?"

He shrugs helplessly.

"That's a pretty big lie to keep up with."

"I know," he says. "I hate lying to them, but I don't want to hurt them, either. This would crush them. I know it would."

I gaze at his profile. "I'm so sorry. I wish there was something I could do."

He turns to me in the low light and smiles in the most breathtaking way. "You've done more than you know." When I frown, he adds, "I haven't talked to anyone about this, outside of Danny and my mom. And then you… I know you won't judge me, or us. You never have."

We fall silent, and it feels peaceful. Safe.

"So that's me," he says. "I'm not hiding anything from you anymore. Because I don't want to. And I don't want you to, either." His gaze drifts over my face. "I really care about you, Eva. I always have. Even when we didn't see each other all that much, I thought about you, and I never stopped caring."

"I care about you, too," I whisper.

"I know this trip has been the worst kind of bad. But we've got each other, right?"

"Yeah," I say softly.

"So, yeah. We'll get through this."

I lean closer to him, taking comfort from his constancy. In the chaos of everything, the doubt and uncertainty, it's *Colton* I am certain of. I'm safe with him, and he's safe with me. And when it's just us, here, alone, everything really does feel like it's going to be okay. Some version of okay, at least.

Before I know it, I'm closer to him. My lips are on his. He falters, just for a moment, but then he kisses me back. His hand rests on the small of my back, and a shiver moves over me.

My head spins as the world dissolves around us. Here, together, this is the only thing I know I'm sure of.

Then the gale slams against the windowpane, making us stop. My eyes shoot to the window, and I see it, a silhouette in the glass. A shadow of a sneering face staring in from outside.

A breath catches in my throat just as the bulb cuts out.

COLTON

Eva takes a sharp breath as the bulb blows, plunging us into darkness.

"It's okay," I say quickly. "It's just the power. The storm must have taken the power out."

"No," she chokes, grabbing my sleeve. "Someone's out there!" Before I can untangle her words, she's on her feet, scrambling across the room toward the back window.

"Who's there?" she yells, flinging open the window to the wild night. The porch bulbs are out, too, and the bay has disappeared in the dark.

I stumble across the room and join her at the window, trying to see out, trying to see what she's seen. But there's nothing but endless black. Eva's shaking, though, leaning against the ledge while she tries to search the night.

"What did you see?"

"There was someone out there watching us," she says, breathing fast. "I'm sure there was."

"What, someone looking in through the window?"

"Yes. I think so." She hesitates and drags her hands through her hair. "I'm sure I saw someone. I thought I did. But…" she trails off and hugs her arms around herself.

I stare at the black pane and whatever lies beyond it.

A bone-cold feeling comes over me. It's too dark to see out. Even if there *is* someone out there, there's no way we'd be able to see them.

EVA

"I should probably go," I murmur into the darkness. I've been lying on Colton's bed for a while with my head rested against his shoulder and nothing but the touch of his hand around mine.

I can't shake the harrowing memory of seeing a sneering face in the window, watching us, taunting us. But I know the night can play cruel tricks with its bending shadows and deceptive shapes. Whatever it was that I saw, or thought I saw, there's nothing I can do about it now. The power is out, and there's nothing to do but wait for the morning to come.

Colton speaks quietly beside me. "You don't have to leave."

"I don't want to," I answer, holding his hand a little tighter. "But Alice… I know she'll be worried after I left the cabin in the way that I did. And Karly, it must be getting late, she won't want to sleep in our room alone."

"Yeah. You're probably right."

"Maybe there's been word from Miles, too." There's optimism in my tone, but I'm not sure I truly believe the words.

Colton's voice comes back to me through the darkness. "Yeah, maybe."

Despite his response, I get the feeling neither of us is holding out much hope. If Miles were back, someone would have told us; they would have come looking for us, surely.

I lean closer into Colton, relishing the warmth in the cold night, the familiar scent of sports spray and salt water.

"Will you be okay?" he asks.

"Yes," I whisper. But my stomach knots. Again, my thoughts wander to the face in the window, the cruel sneer... A trick of my tired and overimaginative mind, I remind myself. I have to keep reminding myself.

"You know I'll be right next door if you need me."

I squeeze his hand. "Thanks. You, too."

"I'll walk you to your room."

He moves, and I move, too. I feel my way through the darkness until my fingers graze the door handle. Outside, the bulbs are all out, and the moonlight is the only guide. I make it to my room and slip inside, leaving Colton alone on the deck.

"Karly?" I call softly as I close the door with a quiet click.

She doesn't respond, but I hear the steady sound of breathing coming from across the room. There's a moment where it crosses my mind, though, the question: *Is it Karly?* But I quickly bury the fear that it could be someone else lying there in her bed. Someone waiting to target me, like they did with Piper, and maybe Miles.

Like it or not, Danny's words, and his paranoia, have taken root.

I forge a path to my side and fumble around the nightstand

for my phone. My fingers bump the smooth case, and I free it from the charger. The bright backlight is jarring, but a comfort in the darkness. The red battery bar, on the other hand, is far from comforting—evidently the power cut out too soon.

I sweep the light across the bedroom and see Karly's ruby-toned hair fanned over her pillow. At the sight, my heart rate normalizes a little. It *is* her, and not some stranger lying in wait.

I bring the screen to eye level and check through my latest messages. Still no reply from Miles.

But there's one from Alice. Where are you? You can't just walk out like that, Eva. We're all worried, we need to stay together.

I type out a response. I'm sorry. I'm back in my room. It's just getting to me, you know?

Then I add, Are you okay? before I hit Send.

There are other messages, too, mostly from my parents updating on road closures, and some from classmates who have obviously gotten word of Piper's accident and want to know what happened. But I don't know how I'm supposed to respond. I don't know where to begin.

My throat feels like it's constricting, and I can't breathe. Piper was here, yesterday, in this very room, sitting cross-legged on the floor as she applied her makeup in the full-length mirror. I can still hear her voice, still smell her smoky perfume lingering.

In the bed opposite, Karly whimpers and rolls over, creaking the old frame.

We were supposed to be home by now, all nine of us, safe in our own beds.

I take a deep breath and gather my spiraling thoughts. Tomorrow, as soon as it gets light, I'm going to search for Miles.

Even if the storm hasn't passed, at least I'll have daylight on my side.

I crawl beneath the comforter and tuck my hands under the pillow for warmth. My eyelids are heavy, and I already feel myself begin to drift, beyond exhausted from this nightmare day.

But then I hear a sound and I'm instantly alert again. The creak of a door—*our* door. I hold my breath in the darkness. A shadow moves, edging into the room.

I snatch my phone from the nightstand and hold up the light. "Alice?" I whisper. "Is that you?"

The silhouette retreats and the door thumps shut.

"Who was that?" My voice comes out loud, and Karly coughs out a breath.

I jump from my bed and hurry across the room with my phone's light swaying wildly over the floorboards.

With a sharp inhale, I fling the door open to nothing but the empty corridor.

EVA

Standing on the deck in the darkness, just listening to the rain hit the planks, I move my light from left to right. I didn't imagine it. This isn't my mind concocting monsters. Maybe seeing the face in Colton's window was a trick of the night, of the shadows. But someone opened our door. They came into our room, and when I moved, they ran. I didn't imagine that.

Breathing hard, I sweep my phone light around the lodge, catching the rain in the beam.

"What's going on?" Karly's out of bed, squinting and hugging a sweatshirt around herself.

"Did you see what happened?" I ask her quickly.

Her brow knits. "What do you mean? What happened?"

"Someone came into our room."

Karly stares blankly back at me, so I start knocking on the doors, all of them. We're the only people here, Paul's car is still gone, which means it must have been one of them.

They start emerging from their rooms, sleepy-eyed, rumpled hair, blinking and cringing away from my flashlight. Karly stays huddled in our open doorway.

I look between them all, wondering if anyone is going to speak and own up to the fact that they just came into our room. Maybe they'll have a perfectly plausible explanation for what they were doing, and why they left so abruptly.

Colton steps out onto the deck, one hand knotted through his tousled hair. From the opposite end of the corridor, Danny comes out of the communal cabin. He's alone, and his brow furrows when my light lands on him.

"What's going on?" Colton's voice sounds throaty, rough, like he's just woken up.

"Someone came into our room," I say calmly. Or as calmly as I can manage under the circumstances.

The deck is silent with everyone's gazes wandering over each other, or me.

"Someone came into our room," I say again as I try to organize my racing thoughts. "Then, when they realized I was awake, they left. Quickly."

Danny steps a little closer and rubs his eyes with the heels of his hands. "What? Who?"

"I don't know!" I say, throwing up my arms. "Hence why we're all standing out here. Isn't anyone going to own up to it?"

When no one replies, I breathe out a laugh.

"I can't believe this," I murmur. "No one is going to admit it?"

Alice lifts her palms. "Hey, don't look at me. I was sleeping."

Noah scrubs a hand through his rumpled hair. "Me, too."

Danny and Colton look at each other, communicating in that silent way that they do.

"Guys, please." My voice sounds hoarse, and I regard each of them, one by one. "Please. This is weirding me out. There's no one else here, it had to have been one of…" I trail off and stare into the darkness, half expecting Miles to pop out from around a corner yelling, *Surprise*. But he doesn't. Only the rain on the rooftop responds with loud, quick pattering.

After a few seconds, Alice comes toward me and threads her arm through mine. "Eva, you're exhausted. We're all exhausted. Maybe you *thought* you heard someone come in, and…"

"I didn't hear anything," Karly adds softly.

I roll my eyes. "Yes. That's because you were sleeping."

"Okay," Noah says, waving his big hands as I pass the flashlight over him. "If it was none of us, it could have been Miles."

Karly shoots me an anxious look. She wraps her arms around herself.

I don't confess that I'd wondered the same thing. I just shake my head. "Miles wouldn't have come into our room, then fled at the first sign of movement. He wouldn't want to scare us like that."

Karly lets out a shrill gasp. "Unless Miles really did kill Piper." She chokes out a strangled sob. "And now he's coming for us."

COLTON

I follow Eva to the communal cabin. It took some time to calm Karly down, and Eva did a pretty good job of convincing her that she'd imagined the whole thing, that she'd most likely dreamed someone came into their room and woke up confused. Karly might have fallen for that, but I didn't. I saw the stricken look on Eva's face when no one confessed to opening her door. That fear was for real.

In the cabin, Eva curls up on one of the couches and gazes at the dying embers of the fire.

I toss another log into the hearth and the flames envelop it, slowly charring the wood.

"I can't believe this, Colton," she murmurs as I take a seat beside her. "Now everyone thinks Miles is on some sort of killing spree?" She turns to me, blinking in the low light of the flickering fire.

"Karly doesn't really believe that," I mutter. "It's late, and she's just tripping out about everything."

Her eyes stray from mine. "Do you believe it?" She picks at a scuff on the couch, avoiding my gaze.

"What, about Miles?" I ask, and she nods. I blow out a breath. "No."

The truth is I don't know what I believe anymore. I just know she needed that answer to be *no*. So that's what I said.

She exhales. "Am I imagining things, Colton?"

I fold my arm around her, and she leans into me. "No," I tell her, moving my thumb over her hair.

She stares at the fire, transfixed by the dancing flames. "Are you just saying *no* to everything because you think it'll make me feel better?"

"No." I smile, and she mirrors it, weakly. But it's there. She rests her head on my shoulder.

This closeness, this familiarity between us, it feels so natural and normal. It catches me for a second. A week ago, Eva and I weren't in this space. I liked her, yeah. I've always liked her. And sometimes I wondered if she could feel the same. But now, this intimacy, this sanctuary, it's giving me something I never knew I needed. Someone who trusts me, entirely, and who I know I can trust in return. I don't want to screw that up, for either of us. Because once it's broken, that trust, it doesn't come back. I learned that the hard way.

When she speaks again, her voice sounds lost. "I could have saved Piper."

I frown at her. "What do you mean?"

"I was in the cave," she carries on distantly. "Twenty-four hours ago. I heard her scream, and I went to look. I didn't see her, I didn't see anyone, so I left. I figured whoever it was had already gone because I heard footsteps leave. So, I just walked away, too." Her golden eyes turn glassy. She takes a breath and blinks the emotion away. Then she returns her attention to the fire.

"It's not your fault, Eva," I tell her, trying to snare her gaze. "It was dark. You didn't see her."

She swallows. "But I found the phone, and I saw the cracked screen. I should have figured something was wrong."

"Why would you? You said it yourself, right? No one would have *assumed* that one of us was capable of this. Otherwise, we wouldn't be here with each other."

She breathes softly, and her fingers thread through mine. She's close to me, leaning into my shoulder.

"Someone did this, though," she says dimly. "One of our friends."

I hold her hand a little tighter, safer. "Yeah." I stare into the fire, watching the flames rise. "Thank you, by the way," I say, my voice raw in this private moment.

She lifts her head. Her eyes shine with the reflection of firelight, and my heart thumps.

"For what?" she asks.

"For trusting me."

She nods, just a small movement. "Of course. Thank you for trusting me, too."

I muster a smile. "I always have."

"Same," she whispers, and I hold her closer as we watch the fire burn.

DANNY: Are you with Eva?

COLTON: Yeah. In the cabin.

DANNY: What's going on? Does she have an idea who came into her room just now?

COLTON: No.

DANNY: Who do you think?

COLTON: No idea. You?

DANNY: It wasn't me.

COLTON: No, I mean, who do you think it was?

DANNY: Don't know. Karly was in the room, too, right?

COLTON: Yeah.

DANNY: Noah?

COLTON: He was asleep. Come here, we'll talk.

DANNY: No. Talk later.

EVA

I stare at the fire, entranced by the erratic flames. The wind is rattling the cabin's windowpanes and batting at the door. I stay close to Colton, savoring his warmth, his comfort.

"Danny's not coming," Colton says, slipping his phone into his pocket.

My gaze stays trained on the dancing flames. "Okay."

"I think it's getting to him, everything."

"It's getting to all of us."

We fall quiet.

I can hear Colton's heartbeat where I'm resting against him, just a steady rhythm.

But in our silence, my thoughts and emotions are anything but steady. I can't shake the echo of Piper's voice. *I'm going to tell everyone what you did.*

Not only that. The memory of the text message she sent when we were at the diner, asking if I knew, it plays on my mind.

"There must be a connection," I mutter to myself.

Colton shifts. His eyes cast downward to meet mine. "A connection between what?"

I sit up straight and shake my head, gathering my thoughts. "On our way here, when we stopped at the diner, Piper texted me just saying *do you know*. What did she think I knew?"

He stares blankly back at me.

"So now I'm wondering," I carry on. "There must be something that connects whatever Piper thought I knew, and whoever she was threatening? But what did she think I knew?"

He stops for a minute, frowns. "Miles and the exam papers?"

"But everyone knew that," I point out. "You said so yourself. What Piper knew obviously wasn't public knowledge, otherwise she couldn't have held it as leverage against whoever she was threatening."

"Maybe she had proof on Miles. He's saying he didn't steal those tests, but maybe she had proof that he did."

I tap my finger on my lips, thinking of Miles, my friend since kindergarten. After all our years of friendship, I know him ridiculously well—at least, I thought I did. "Why would Miles steal test papers?" I muse out loud. "He didn't need money or grades. His life was perfectly on track."

Colton doesn't respond.

"I just can't wrap my head around any reality where Miles would sell exam papers," I carry on. "For one thing, it suited him to out-score everyone else in our grade. It gave *him* the advantage."

My eyes stray back to the fire, and the logs that are all but burned out. A piece of the puzzle is still missing, I'm sure of it. I'm just not sure what that piece is.

Then something catches my gaze, something buried in the feathery cinders that have settled in the base of the fireplace. I sit bolt upright, and Colton stares at me, confused. But I'm not looking at him. I can't tear my eyes away from the tiny scrap of familiar material hidden in the remains of the fire, almost disappearing among the silver ashes.

Why is the stone gray top that Piper loved so much now disintegrated in the hearth?

EVA

"What's wrong?" Colton presses.

I untangle myself from him, then stand from the couch and step closer to the fire. "I think..." I crouch before the hearth. "Piper loved this top. Why would someone have thrown it into the fire?"

I glance back at Colton, and he shakes his head, confused.

He's not the only one. My mind is jumbled with questions. "I need to talk to Karly," I say quickly, and I spring to my feet.

Colton follows my lead.

"I'll talk to her alone," I tell him. "But will you be in your room if I knock on your door later?"

"Yeah." He hesitates and frowns. "Are you okay?"

"Yes," I answer with a nod. "You're just going to have to trust me. I'll explain everything once I've made sense of it myself."

"Okay," he agrees after another second.

Together, we start for the front door, our footsteps tapping swiftly over the floorboards.

Out in the corridor, the rain has finally stopped, leaving behind pools on the ground, but the wind still howls through the trees. Across the clearing, Karly's Prius and the Demarcos' truck glisten in the moonlight.

"Still no sign of Paul's car," I say.

Colton's eyes search the darkness, but he stays silent.

We navigate a path back to our rooms using the light from our phones. In the corridor, I rise to my tiptoes and kiss him before we part ways. I haven't told him where my mind has wandered. I need to prove that my hunch is right before I throw anyone's name under the bus. So, I let him walk away, and I return to my own room alone.

Karly is sleeping soundly in her bed, her long red hair curled around the pillow.

I lower my light to the floorboards and cross to her side.

Piper's phone had been right here, in this room. Someone undoubtedly wanted that incriminating video gone before it could be handed over to the police.

Because someone did something that they wanted to stay hidden.

I crouch at Karly's bed and gently touch her shoulder. She wakes with a small gasp and clutches the covers tightly to her chest.

"Sorry," I whisper. "It's just me."

"What's wrong?" she says into the darkness.

"We need to talk," I murmur. "Piper's phone is missing."

She blinks back at me. "What do you mean?"

"Did you or Alice put it somewhere, or take it after I left the room to talk to Danny?"

Her brow furrows. "*I* didn't. I don't know about Alice. I didn't see her take it."

I exhale slowly. "Before I realized Miles had gone, I was looking for Piper's phone. I couldn't find it." I pause and swallow my nerves. "I think Danny might have taken it."

Karly grips the sheet a little tighter. "Oh, my god, Eva..."

"I think he wanted to get rid of the evidence." As I say the words, I cringe. There's only a thin wall between our room and theirs, and I don't know how far my voice will carry.

Karly sits upright, untangling herself from the bedcovers. "We have to call the police," she says. "Danny could be dangerous." She lets out a shattered breath. "He *is* dangerous, clearly."

My pulse starts to quicken as I hold her gaze, preparing to plant a seed that I hope will sprout the way I want it to. "There's more."

She presses her hands to her mouth, just waiting.

"I went back to the cave after we did, just to check my theory one more time, and I found something. A piece of torn material. It's gray, and I think it was part of Piper's top, that one that she loved from the online store."

Her eyebrows draw together, and she shakes her head. "I don't understand."

"I was in the common room with Colton, and a bit of that very same material caught my eye—almost turned completely to ash in the fire. There might have been DNA on it," I explain. "If there was some sort of altercation and Piper's top ripped in the scuffle, then DNA from Danny's fingernails might still be on that material. Why else would someone want to destroy it? This could prove that he was the person who pushed her that night. Because whoever tried to burn it—they didn't get all of it."

Karly's eyes turn glassy in the low light. "Where is it?" she murmurs. "Where's the material now?"

"I left it exactly where it was, I didn't want to contaminate it with my DNA. I know it's late, but it's high tide soon, so I just called the police so that the forensic team can collect it and do whatever they need to do. They're on their way."

She gives a shaky nod. "Okay."

"We just have to get through tonight, Karly."

She nods again. "Yeah."

"I'm going to try to get some sleep," I tell her, standing. "Sorry for waking you, I just had to update you."

"Yeah," she whispers. "Thanks."

I retreat to my side and crawl into my bed, pulling the covers around me. I force my eyes shut, but my mind is whirling.

COLTON

Danny is sitting on the edge of his bed when I come in. The shadowed sight of him catches me off guard.

"Hey. You're still awake?"

"Yeah," he rasps.

The sound of his voice makes me stop. I track my flashlight over him. His knee is bouncing, and his fists are balled.

It takes one look. One look, and my heart starts hammering in my chest.

"What's going on?"

He doesn't answer.

I start breathing harder. "What did you do?"

"Nothing." He's breathing fast, too. His hands keep opening and closing, twitching.

"Come on, Danny." My pulse is thundering in my ears. "You're lying."

"I'm not," he brushes me off. He turns away, looking at the wall, the door, the window.

I drag my hand over my mouth. "Yes, you are. You're lying. What have you done?"

"I...haven't." His voice is hoarse, ragged. "I didn't..."

I feel as though the breath has been knocked right out of my lungs. I can barely bring myself to say the words. "Danny. Did you kill Piper?"

He gets up and strides across the room, shouldering past me. Before I can stop him, he's out the door.

EVA

I keep my eyes closed, focusing only on controlling my breathing. Everything about this room seems strange to me. The unfamiliar smells and the feel of the rough cotton pillowcase on my cheek. The way the wind whistles through the gaps, taking on a voice of its own.

I can hear Miles's words in my mind as I lie still in my bed, breathing steadily into the pillow.

I didn't do it.

The news of Miles's expulsion worked its way around school fast. Students formed clusters in the hallway to watch him pack up his locker. People we knew, people we didn't know. It was a sight to behold. The school's A-star senior student, all lined up for valedictorian and Ivy League prospects, packing up his locker after getting caught cheating, and profiting from it. His parents walked stiffly from the principal's office. His mom's hand was covering her mouth. His dad was tense and pale.

I think of Miles casually using Mr. Harris's computer, knowing the admin password by heart. Teachers trusted him. Because he was trustworthy. He *is* trustworthy.

And his words keep echoing.

I think I saw something I wasn't supposed to see.

I didn't do it.

Someone set me up.

That day in Mr. Harris's classroom, when Miles's computer crashed, he logged on to the system as admin to recover his assignment. I was with him, and I don't remember him logging off after he'd finished. We just walked right out and went to lunch.

Danny was in the classroom that day, too, working on a group project. He was there when Miles packed up his locker as well, standing among the crowd. I saw the look on Danny's face—that stunned, frozen expression. At the time, I thought it was because he was feeling the same way I was, totally shocked. And he was, but for him, maybe that feeling hit a little differently.

Then when Piper texted me at the diner, wondering if I knew something. And the way she kept bringing up Miles's situation, making everyone feel uncomfortable. It wasn't that people were uncomfortable talking about a friend's downfall—at least, that wasn't the case for all of us. It was because someone had something to hide, and Piper knew it.

When we first arrived at the lodge, and I challenged Piper on the text message she'd sent at the diner, she looked at Colton.

At least, that's what I'd thought. But Colton had been standing with Miles and Danny.

I hear the click of our door opening, and my blood turns to ice.

EVA

I wait, holding as still as I can beneath the bed covers, breathing slowly, steadily, and counting away the seconds in my mind.

One second, two seconds, three... I listen for the footsteps in the corridor outside the room. One set of footsteps turns to two. Voices, murmurs, breaths.

But I stay silent, just listening. And then, when I can't hear them anymore, I climb out of bed and cross the room. I fumble into my coat and boots and step out into the endless expanse of night.

I tread softly along the corridor and tap on the door neighboring mine. When there's no response, I twist the handle. The room is dark, and both the beds are empty. I take an unsteady breath as I close the door. Then I keep walking along the deck and around the side of the building.

I guess I'm doing this alone.

COLTON

I follow Danny along the waterlogged road, trudging through thick mud. The rain has stopped, but the ground is flooded, and the wind still drives hard at the trees that flank the track.

"So, what?" I call to him, my flashlight jumping. "You're just going to leave?" I hold the beam of light in the space between us, following his sunken footprints in the mud.

He stops for a beat, but he doesn't turn around. My light lands on his back, and the backpack slung over his shoulder.

I stop, too. "No explanation? No nothing. You're just going to leave in the middle of the night like Miles did?"

He won't speak. He won't turn around to face me.

"Don't you think I deserve an explanation?" I call to him. "I'm your brother."

His shoulders are hunched forward, head dipped down, fingers gripped around the bag's strap. "I'm running," he murmurs to the night.

My heart thumps. "Where are you running to?"

"Anywhere I can't be found."

I choke out a laugh. "You'll *get* found. Trust me, Danny, you won't make it far. The cops will be looking for a murderer."

That did it. It must have been the word *murderer*, because at that he finally turns to face me. His tortured expression brings a painful pressure to my chest.

My phone's light catches half his face, leaving the other half lost in shadow.

"Colton." His voice sounds scratchy, raw. "I did something really bad."

EVA

Two of them.

Two of them.

I see them a little way ahead, walking side by side across the bay. They're heading for the cave. Her long hair stirs in the wind.

I'd expected Karly from the moment I saw the last remains of her beloved silver-gray top buried in the ashes of the fire. A top she'd specifically told Piper she'd wear that night.

I'd expected Karly. But I'd naively assumed she'd be alone.

I follow their light across the cove, keeping enough of a distance to ensure that they can't see me or hear my footsteps behind them, but close enough that I don't lose their light. Not that I need light to know where they're going. I know because I laid the trap, and they took the bait.

Except my foolproof plan hasn't quite gone off without a hitch because Colton and Danny weren't in their room. Without them, I'm alone. Regardless, I'm going to prove who killed Piper. If I don't keep going, keep following them through the howling wind, then my lie about finding material in the cave will be wasted. I might only have one shot at this before she—*they*—get suspicious.

I cling a little tighter to my phone, hoping the battery holds out long enough to make this work.

Their light and silhouettes disappear into the mouth of the cave, and I quicken my pace to catch up with them. I hold my breath, moving carefully over the rocks, trying not to make a sound. With my pulse racing, I edge closer to the hollow and press myself against the rock wall. The feel of the tide pools beneath my shoes takes me right back to that night.

I'd heard stones clicking that night when someone fled the cave. One set of footsteps. Two.

I see them now, searching the cave, two beams of light running over the ground and dank walls as they scramble for the piece of material that doesn't exist.

They haven't noticed me, and they're muttering between one another.

"Just look everywhere…" she says in a clipped voice.

"What's the point?" he says, moving his light over the damp, rocky ground. "It could have been washed away by now."

"I'm not taking that chance. Are you?"

I stand motionless in the darkness, letting myself be invisible. My phone is set to record, and the seconds are ticking slowly by. I just need them to slip up, to say it. Say that they killed Piper.

Because, of course, they had to have been together. They

were the only ones left at the fire. They were each other's alibi. Everyone else had gone: Me, Miles, Alice, Danny, Colton, Javier...

Until only three remained. Piper, Karly, and Noah.

"I can't see anything," Noah says.

"Just keep looking," Karly hisses.

I edge my phone higher, hoping the recording is picking up their words. I need the sound to be caught clearly if I want this video to count for anything.

Noah is crouched a short distance from me, searching around a tide pool. I press myself flat to the cave wall and the jagged rock face digs into my spine.

All of a sudden, the wind rolls a pebble into the mouth of the cave, scraping it along the ground. I hold my breath as Noah stands to full height and turns to trace the sound. His flashlight hits me, and I shield my eyes from the glare.

"Eva," he says, freezing. "Shit. What are you...?" He glances at Karly. "What are you doing out here?"

Karly spins around to face me, and her eyes widen.

I try to speak, but when I see Karly's expression, I realize there's no point.

Her lips part, because we both know, we *all* know, that none of us can lie our way out of this. She stumbles forward, steadying herself on the wall, and an exhale falls from her.

I see it in her haunted stare—she knows I lied about the material. And I know she lied about everything.

I steel myself. Oh, well. I guess I'm all in now.

"You killed Piper." My words rebound in the hollow.

Noah barks out a laugh. "What? What are you talking about, Eva?"

"Is that it?" I murmur, raising an eyebrow. "Aren't you going to try to convince me that it was Danny? Or Miles?"

"What?" Noah flounders. "That's... You're losing it, Eva."

"I'm not the one looking for a hoax piece of evidence in a cave in the middle of the night."

They both fall silent.

"How could you do this?" I breathe. "You killed Piper."

"We didn't do anything," Karly exclaims.

But I don't stop, I can't. "And to Javier? He's your best friend, Noah. How could you set him up for something you did?"

"I never said it was Javier," Noah bites back.

"Oh, that's right. You're trying to pin it on Danny."

Karly sucks air through her teeth. "Danny isn't as innocent as you think he is, Eva."

And just like that, the final piece of the puzzle falls into place for me. The piece that I was missing.

It takes me a moment to allow it to sink in, to truly believe it. "That day in Mr. Harris's classroom..." The words catch in my throat. "You were all there, you two and Danny. Miles logged on to the server, and you all saw."

They look at each other.

Karly forces a strained laugh. "What?"

"You were all in on it. All three of you." My chest constricts with anger, sadness. Both. "I can't believe I didn't see this." My mind floods with memories of Piper, and the way they'd all squirm whenever she brought up Miles's expulsion. Piper had this over them. She wanted them to know that she could ruin their lives with the snap of her fingers. Just like how they ruined Miles's life.

I meet Karly's eyes in the light from Noah's phone. "You made the mistake of telling Piper?"

"I didn't tell Piper anything!" she cries. "That was Danny!"

Noah shoots her a glower, his strong jaw clenched, warning her to stop talking. But it's too late, I heard it. And so did my phone.

Noah brings his attention back to me, sandy-blond curls moving in the night wind. "Eva," he says calmly, "I don't know what you *think* you've figured out here, but—"

"Then let me explain," I interrupt. "You guys were selling test papers." I hold steady under their shadowed stares, despite the fear rushing through me in bolts. "You two and Danny. And when it came out, you blamed it on Miles because he was traceable, right? Miles was the one who logged on to the server, but *you* downloaded the files."

"Eva, please." Karly takes a step forward, her arm outstretched toward me. I stumble back, and my shoe slaps into a pool. "Listen to me," she says, quickly. "We didn't blame anything on Miles. The downloads were traced back to the time he recovered his own assignment from the system and the school drew their own conclusion—"

"Karly," Noah says through his teeth. "*Shut* your goddamn mouth."

Their faces morph in the bouncing light, bending shadows and distorting features. Karly, with her eyes wide and frantic, and her long hair wild and tangled by the gale. Noah, the muscles in his jaw bulging and his biceps tensed. I don't recognize them. I don't want to recognize them.

I swallow my fear. "So, Danny told Piper," I forge on, "and she was holding this over you all. You killed her to keep her quiet, so that your lives and futures wouldn't be ruined by this?"

Right away, I know that I've made a mistake. I must have moved my hand without realizing it because Noah's eye dart down to my phone.

I stumble backward as he takes a step closer to me.

"I'm going to need that," he says, reaching for my phone. I scramble away from him, slipping on the slick rocks, but I'm not fast enough, and he pries the phone from my hand. I watch, helplessly, as he taps on the screen.

"Deleted," he says, and my stomach rolls. Then he launches my cell into the night, and I hear it plop into the ocean beyond the cave.

The way that they look at me then, their eyes sunken in the light, there's something almost remorseful, regretful. But I know it's not about what they've done. It's about what they're about to do.

I try to run, but Noah's big hand seals around my arm. Karly takes my other arm, and they force me to the ground in the space between them.

"You can't do this," I yell.

"We have no choice," Karly whispers.

It's funny, really. Noah's over six feet tall, muscular and solid, but it's Karly's grip that hurts the most.

COLTON

"What did you do, Danny? Did you kill her?"

We're standing face-to-face on the flooded road with the trees groaning and bowing around us.

"No." His voice is shaking. He's shaking. "I didn't, I swear." He hesitates and swallows. "But I think I know who did."

The cold wind steals the air from my lungs.

His words come out too fast. "Miles wasn't selling papers. It was me."

I can't speak. I can't think.

"Noah, Karly, and me," he says. "We found the exams on the server. We downloaded them to score some extra cash."

"Danny." My breath is ragged. "Please tell me you're joking?"

He rubs his sleeve over his eyes. "I needed the money," he rasps. "For college."

"I had it under control!" I shout. "I've got the money."

"Yeah, for *me*." He slaps his hand to his chest. "You had the money for *me*, not you."

I close my eyes and shake my head.

"I didn't think we'd get traced," he says, tripping over his words. "I had no idea this would come back on Miles, and when it did, I wanted to come clean. I tried to so many times, but we agreed."

My mind is working too fast, trying to make sense of what he's telling me. "Noah was in on this, too?"

He nods, and his jaw twitches.

"Noah doesn't even need the money," I say in a breath.

"But he needed the grades."

I trap my lip between my teeth. "I can't believe you," I murmur. "Miles is your best friend."

"I didn't know it would come back on him! If I'd known, I never would have—"

"But you did know." I aim my finger at him. "You did. After. And you still let him take the fall."

He grimaces. "You think that didn't kill me inside? You think it isn't *still* killing me? I told Piper because I couldn't stand the…" He gives way to a rough breath. "The guilt was tearing me up, Colton. I had to talk to someone."

"Me." I press my fist to my chest. "You should have come to me, and I would have told you to do the right thing."

"Exactly," he says. Then he lowers his voice. "That's why I *didn't* come to you." There's no pride in his words. There's no pride in any of this.

I scrub my hands through my hair. "Danny…"

"When you and Eva told me about that video on Piper's phone," he says, "I had this feeling it was Karly or Noah, because of everything that's gone on, right? I didn't think of it before, but the video, and what Piper said that night…" he trails off and exhales. "One of them killed Piper, and they're going to set me up for it."

"They wouldn't—"

"Of course, they would! You heard the way Karly threatened me in the cabin earlier. She said in front of everyone she thought it was me or you, because she wanted me to know that she was going to play that hand." He stops and looks dead into my eyes. "I've got to run, Colton."

I hold his stare. "Don't."

"Come with me," he says, blinking fast. "We'll be okay together. We'll figure it out, like we always do."

I don't answer. Because he already knows, if he goes, I'll go with him.

Somewhere in the distance, a sound travels on the wind. Almost like a scream on the keening gale.

I halt, listening to the night, the rustle of wind through the forest, the crash of the ocean somewhere farther away.

"Did you hear that?" I ask Danny.

He frowns back at me. "Hear what?"

EVA

The piercing sound of Alice's scream makes them stop. Makes us all stop.

"Let go of her!" Alice cries.

Karly and Noah falter just long enough for me to slip free from them, and I scramble to my feet.

But Noah blocks my path. "Alice…" he says.

"What were you doing to her?" Alice's words are frantic. Her flashlight bounces around the cave, spinning over us. "What are you all doing out here?"

I summon my voice, but it's too quiet, lost in the crashing tide. "Alice, help—"

"Alice," Karly cries over me. "Eva killed Piper. You have to get out to the road and call the police, get help."

"What?" I stammer. "No. That isn't—"

"Alice, listen to me." Noah's voice is deep, and his hands are outstretched, raised to show that he's no threat to her. "Eva

killed Piper. We caught her trying to get rid of evidence. Get
to the road and call the police."

"No," I try again.

But Alice just looks between them, breathing erratically.
Two against one, and they're putting on the performance of a
lifetime. Karly's arms are folded tightly, and tears are streaming down her cheeks. Noah is cool, calm, collected. And then
there's me, stunned and unable to string a sentence together,
even though my life depends on it.

Alice's gaze lands on Karly, and Karly manages a weak nod.

"Noah's telling the truth," she says. "We lied and told Eva
we'd found evidence here, and she came to get rid of it. That's
how we know it was her."

My stomach lurches. I see the fear in Alice's eyes when she
looks at me.

"We think she's done something to Miles, too," Noah
jumps in. "That fight they had in your room, and then we
couldn't find Eva, she went after him…"

My breath hitches.

Alice's eyes glisten as she turns back to Karly.

"She fooled all of us," Karly whispers hoarsely.

"Call the police," Noah shouts. "Go!"

In a desperate attempt to reach her, I cross my first two
fingers—*our* sign—hoping that she'll remember. Hoping that
through all of this, through all of the horrors and lies, Alice
will remember who I am.

But she turns and bolts from the cave.

I choke out a strangled sound. "No, Alice! Wait!"

My voice echoes in the hollow.

And just like that, we're alone again.

EVA

When I was twelve years old, my dad bought me a surfboard. I wiped out every time I tried to ride it. And every time, I'd swim back into shore, frustrated and ready to give up, and he'd just smile, tell me I was doing great, and help me get back on.

I don't know why that's the moment I'm thinking of right now. Maybe it's because I'm so close to the water and the waves. I can taste the salt in the air. I can feel the spray from the ocean on my skin.

Or maybe it's because I know that if I give up now, then it's over.

They're blocking the mouth of the cave, and they swap a look. I see it clearly—the exact moment where they decide it's them or me. The tension in Noah's jaw, and the fragile nod from Karly.

I glance through the gaping jaws of the cave to the rocky outcropping hanging over the ocean while I imagine the many ways this can end for me. There's a fleeting moment where I almost surrender and accept whatever fate has in store for me.

But then I snap myself out of it—I'm not done yet. I cast one more glance to the night beyond the mouth of the cave, and I nod.

Let's go.

"Karly." My voice is clear now, controlled. "Karly, listen to me." I step closer to her and take her cold hands in mine. The tears in her eyes are real, because she's scared. She's guilty and looking for a lifeline. I get it because I'm in the same boat. "We can pin all of this on Noah," I tell her, and he scoffs. But Karly's listening, her eyes stay on me, so I keep going. "There's no way anyone would believe you killed Piper. She was your best friend."

Noah snorts. "Nice try, Eva."

"Danny will vouch for Noah selling the papers. This could *all* be on Noah," I whisper, gripping Karly's hands tighter. "No one would think you had anything to do with this. You're not strong enough to overpower Piper."

"Whoa." Noah cuts in, holding his palms up. "You think she's not strong enough? Karly was the one who pushed her, not me."

Karly's eyes snap to him. "Don't do that." She's spitting venom, glaring at him through the darkness. "You were there, too. You might not have pushed her, but you wanted to scare her as much as I did. You didn't help her after she fell." Her eyes jump back to me, ghostly in the wavering light still coming from Noah's phone. "We didn't know the tide was coming in. Piper must have hit her head, and…" More tears roll down her face. "Eva, please, you have to believe me. We never meant to kill her." The words are just broken sobs. Her trembling hands cling helplessly to mine.

"I do believe you," I tell her. "Of course I do." I can feel Noah's stare on me, but I don't break eye contact with Karly. I can't. "Think about it," I say to her. "We could walk away from this. It'll be our secret. Just you, me, and Danny."

"I didn't mean for her to die," she whimpers. "Noah and I, we just took her aside to talk."

"Shut up, Karly," he says through his teeth. "*Stop* talking."

"Piper kept dropping hints about Miles," Karly carries on breathlessly. "About the papers, and secrets. She kept hinting about it on her *goddamn* Instagram Stories."

"I know," I say. "I noticed. It's understandable that you wanted her to stop threatening you and taunting you with this. I get it."

Karly nods quickly. "We just wanted to talk to her when we finally had a minute alone, and then we got into a huge fight. She said she'd tell everyone, and it just happened."

Noah aims an index finger at her. "*You* did it, not me."

"*You* tricked her into coming to the cave, talking about a photo shoot," she says with a ragged breath.

I glance at Noah. "It was you who came into our room earlier, wasn't it? Because, what, you were trying to manipulate Karly?" I see his teeth clench, but I need to divide them if I want any chance of getting out of this alive. I need to get Karly on my side.

"He thought I was alone," Karly whispers. "When Javier got arrested, Noah felt bad and said we should work together to shift the blame onto Danny. He had a plan—"

"We can put this all on Noah," I say quickly. "I'm down if you are, Karly. Just say the word."

But she doesn't get a chance to speak because Noah lunges for me.

COLTON

When Noah moves in on Eva, that's when I intervene.

They've told us enough now, anyway.

After I heard the scream, Danny and I sprinted down to the cove from the road, following the movement of flashlight coming from the cave.

I know she saw us. Eva. Well, she saw me, at least, standing behind Noah and Karly, just outside the cave's entrance. She signaled to me with a nod, and I got it. I pushed my hand against Danny's chest, and we stayed still, hidden by the darkness. Silently, we listened to every word. And I kept recording, even after I pulled Noah off her.

EVA

I fall against Colton's chest, and he holds me close, wrapping his arms around me. Noah and Karly stagger backward, their eyes jumping between Danny, Colton, and me. The stunned expressions on their faces buy us time, an extra moment to figure out our next move.

"Go," Colton says to me. He slips his phone into my hands. "Go. Call the cops."

So, I do. I run from the cave. My shoes sink heavily into the sand, and I stumble with every step, but I don't stop. I cling to the phone, which, if Colton managed to record everything, contains enough evidence to expose Noah and Karly.

I race for the lodge, and I don't look back.

Up ahead, a beam of light moves on the deck. It nears the beach and I see Alice galloping down the stone steps. We almost collide into one another.

She grabs my arm. "I've called the police," she cries. "They're on their way."

"No, Alice, please," I say, breathlessly. My lungs feel like they're on fire. "It wasn't me."

"I know," she jumps in, gently squeezing my arm. "I didn't believe them. But I didn't think we'd be able to overpower them, so I came back here to get cell service and called the police. I passed Colton and Danny on my way back and warned them." She hugs me quickly. "Where are they all?"

I turn and look back into the darkness. There's no light in the cove. No sound of footsteps or voices. "Colton and Danny." I scan the night. "I thought they were right behind me." I grip Alice's hand, scared. Because I can't see any of them anymore.

Noah, Karly, Colton, or Danny.

COLTON

Noah slams his palms into my chest, and I fall backward into the water. It's ice-cold, and the current pulls me under. My skull clips against a rock, and everything spins as I fight to get to the surface. It takes me back to all those winters, with Noah and Javier. The rush as we jumped off the bluff and hit the water so hard it stung.

But we always came back up.

I break through to the surface and suck in a lungful of air. My head's spinning, and I grope the water for anything I can hold on to as the current tries to pull me back under. Noah is on the rock projection, standing above me in the moonlight. For a second, I think he's reaching out to grasp my hand, to pull me up onto the ledge, just like I did for him when we were here before. But when I grab the rock at his feet, he boots my hand, and my fingers slip from the stone.

A wave curls over me, forcing me under and dragging me

farther out. I'm barely keeping my head above water. My skull is throbbing, and my vision is blinking in and out while I feel myself start to lose consciousness. Moving beams of light. Noah, Karly, Danny.

I think he's shouting for me. Danny. He's tracking his phone's light over the water. He can't see me.

And I'm being thrown around. Under. Up. Under. Breathe.

Then he's running to the edge of the projection.

I hold my breath one last time as the current drags me under.

PIPER

Hey, guys. It's just me, Piper, here for some real talk.

So, here's the thing. I guess I'm on a journey of personal growth right now, and I want to share my story with you. Something I want you all to know about me is that I'm a total empath. I just get a vibe off people, like I can see who they truly are beneath the bullshit. Know what I mean?

Okay, I have an example for you. Imagine someone did a really bad thing, something straight-up unforgiveable, but they felt it inside, like it physically hurt them to know they'd morally effed up, right? Those people eventually will put it right because, I don't know, they just have to. If they don't, it'll eat away at them forever. It's just how they're built.

But then there are the other types of people. The people

who could do the exact same bad thing, and not give a shit. Like truly not give a shit.

Listen, guys, I'm not saying I'm perfect. I'm not saying I've never done anything bad, but I know the difference between right and wrong.

So, I guess I'm on this journey, recognizing and weeding out all the toxic people in my life. And I just want to put a message out there to the second group of people, the shady-ass people who don't give a shit about what they've done. It's going to come out. The truth. Eventually. Karma will catch up with you one day, and let me tell you, it's going to bite.

Just wait.

COLTON

He's okay. That's the first thing I remember hearing after they pulled me out of the water. And I remember seeing them, all of them. Not Karly or Noah—they were gone—but the other three: Danny, Eva, and Alice. They were standing over me, crowded around me and checking me over with a flashlight as I coughed and spun out.

We're okay. I remember thinking it. Knowing it. And I was right.

The sun is bright this afternoon. It's as though last night never happened. The storm, the wild coast, and the water-logged roads, it's all gone, and we're nearly home.

Javier's in the front passenger seat, next to me. He slept through most of the ride, but he's coming to now. His arm is slung over his face and he's squinting against the sunlight streaming through the windshield. The police let him go this morning—they let us all go. Paul got back to the lodge in the early hours, around the same time we did. His car had gotten stuck on the flooded road, and he walked back through the forest. The police got to us soon after that, and we told them everything. Karly and Noah were found trying to hitch a ride out of town a couple of hours later.

Danny, Eva, and Alice are in the back seat, talking quietly between themselves. I glance at them in the mirror every now and then, and I feel this gripping relief that we're all together, alive.

Steering onto my street, I pull up along the curb outside my house. I cut the engine and lean back in my seat, my hands still resting on the wheel.

"Oh, my god!" Eva breathes from the back. She untangles herself from her seat belt and flings the truck door open. It takes me a second to catch up, but then I see him. Miles. He's sitting on the stoop outside our house.

When he sees Eva racing toward him, he stands, grins, and Eva throws her arms around his neck. Alice is close behind. Even Javier jumps out of the truck to greet him.

I hear their tearful reunion from the open window, and a smile tugs at my lips.

In the back seat, Danny takes a slow breath.

We managed to get through to Miles's phone in the morning. He made it to the road late last night and caught a bus back to Seattle from there. Apparently, his head was all over the place when he left, and he couldn't cope with the paranoia and cabin fever. During the call, we told him everything. *Danny* told him everything—about Piper, Karly, Noah, and his involvement in selling the test papers. On the call, Miles went quiet after that. I figure he was processing it all. He was hurt, probably. But I think he'll forgive Danny faster than Danny will forgive himself.

I don't know what the consequences will be for Danny, but I know he'll take them, whatever they are. Karly and Noah will have to face what they did, too. According to Paul, they've confessed to everything and will be awaiting trial.

"Are you going?" I ask Danny, nodding toward the stoop where the others are still knotted together.

"Yeah," he murmurs. He takes a deep breath. "Yeah."

The back door opens with a creak, and Danny gets out onto the pavement. Slowly.

I follow behind him. He heads for the house, with his hands stuffed into his jacket pockets.

Suddenly, Miles's eyes are on Danny. Everyone's eyes are on him.

"I'm sorry," Danny says. There's a catch in his voice.

Miles nods. "I know you are."

EVA

Fortunately, school's been out for spring break this past week, otherwise I don't know how I would have survived fielding all the questions. I've tried my best to keep up with calls and text messages, with everyone wondering what happened on the trip, but I think we all needed a minute to get our heads around it. I'm still not quite there, but I'm getting closer day by day.

Piper's memorial is tonight, and judging by the response on social media, there's going to be a huge turnout. Alice has been working on a portrait to be displayed in school commemorating Piper, and everyone from our grade has rallied. I hope we can do Piper justice. Her life deserves to be celebrated, like she would have wanted it to be.

The sound of the doorbell chimes through the house. From the den, I listen to my dad's footsteps in the hallway and his buoyant greeting at the door.

"Hello!" he says brightly. "Come on in. It's good to see you. How are you?"

I hear a familiar voice respond, and I sit up a little higher on the couch. "I'm alright, thank you, Mr. Porta. How are you?"

I haven't seen Colton since he dropped me off at my house last Sunday. When he hugged me goodbye that day, a lump formed in my throat. I don't know if it was from the relief of being home, the grief around what had transpired, sheer exhaustion kicking in, or the emotion around saying goodbye to Colton. Or perhaps a messy combination of everything. But when the door closed behind him, and I heard his truck pull out onto the street, I burst into tears. And it was a while before I stopped crying.

The days have been lost in a whirlwind since then, a jumble of police, reporters, and friends, and I guess we all needed time to recover. But I've thought about Colton. A lot.

"Eva's right through here." Dad's voice sounds nearer now, and the den's door handle twists. I stand and knot my hands as Dad and Colton appear in the doorway. Dad smiles broadly, his eyes crinkling at the corners. Colton's hands are stuffed into his jacket pockets and his lips are pressed together into a reticent smile.

"Hi," he says.

"Hi," I echo.

Dad claps Colton's shoulder. "I'll give you two some privacy," he says.

I manage to find my voice. "Thanks, Dad."

But before he leaves, he shakes Colton's hand. "Eva told me about how you looked out for her in Oregon," he adds in earnest. "Thank you for that."

Colton's nose twitches. "Of course," he says, clearing his throat. "Always. She looked out for me, too."

"Glad to hear it." Dad gives me a nod as he leaves the room, closing the door behind him with a quiet click.

And just like that, Colton and I are alone for the first time since the lodge. His eyes wander over the den, taking it all in. "You guys redecorated. Nice."

A laugh escapes me. "Good observation, considering you haven't been in this room since we were kids. We've probably redecorated a couple of times since then."

He grins. "I notice things."

I smile back. "How've you been?"

"Alright." He runs a hand over his mouth. "Danny and my mom have been working through some stuff, so home is better than it has been in a while."

I touch my heart. "That's great, Colton."

"Yeah. It's going to take some time, but we'll get there. I've got some plans for college, too," he says. "Maybe not this year, but next year, for sure."

"I'm so pleased for you," I tell him, honestly. "And how's Javier?"

Colton draws in a long breath. "Up and down, you know?"

"Of course. Tell him I'm thinking of him?"

"I will." He pauses and his eyes linger on mine. "How about you?"

I consider it for a moment. "I'm okay," I answer at last. "It's been a lot, but…"

"Yeah," he says, quietly. "I know."

My pulse quickens as I hold his gaze. "I've missed you," I blurt out.

His eyes don't move from mine. "I've missed you, too," he murmurs.

He takes a step closer to me, and I practically fall into him. His arms fold around me and he hugs me tightly, his heart slowly thudding against mine.

In this moment, after everything that's happened, Colton still feels like the safest place to me. A constant in an ever-changing world. I don't know what the future holds for us, for any of us, but I know that I have Colton, and he has me.

I rise to my tiptoes and kiss him. Butterflies rush through me because I'm realizing with every breath, every heartbeat, every kiss that we're so lucky.

This is just the beginning for us.

★ ★ ★ ★ ★

ACKNOWLEDGMENTS

Bad Like Us wouldn't be complete without the help of so many incredible people…

To my wonderful agent, Whitney Ross, whose guidance and support is invaluable. I'm so lucky to have you in my corner!

Thanks to Melissa Frain for editing this book in its early stages and bringing out the best (and worst!) in these characters.

Huge thanks to Meghan McCullough for the editorial magic and fantastic advice along the way. And to the Inkyard Press/HarperCollins team for all the work that went into this project. Bess Braswell, Brittany Mitchell, Justine Sha, Dana Francoeur, and everyone who helped shape and promote this book.

Thanks to my wonderful parents, Angela and Elio, whose kindness, patience, and support is endless!

Thanks to my husband, James, and my children, Sophia and Hayden, who fill our home with laughter and smiles.

Thanks to my sister, Natalie, and brother-in-law Rhodri

for all your help. Natalie, if you've made it to this page then the scary parts are over!

Thanks to my family and friends for your support over the years: Lepores, Nelsons, Shirley, Carters, Roger, Trisha, Sue, Chimbwandas, Nan, Nikki, Lorna, Louis.

Finally, heartfelt thanks to *you* for choosing *Bad Like Us*! I hope you enjoyed it, and I hope it kept you guessing!